ANIMORPHS

The Capture

K.A. Applegate

Hippo

For Michael

Scholastic Children's Books,
Commonwealth House, 1 – 19 New Oxford Street, London WC1A 1NU, UK
a division of Scholastic Ltd
London ~ New York ~ Toronto ~ Sydney ~ Auckland

First published in the USA by Scholastic Inc., 1997
First published in the UK by Scholastic Ltd, 1997

ISBN 0 590 19643 X

Printed by Cox & Wyman Ltd, Reading, Berks.

10 9 8 7 6 5 4 3 2 1

Chapter 1

I'm Jake.

Just Jake. You don't need to know my last name, and I can't tell you, anyway. My story is full of small lies. I've changed people's names. I've changed the names of places. I've changed small details here and there.

But the big stuff is true.

All of it.

The Yeerks are here. On Earth. That is true.

The Yeerks have made Controllers of many humans. They have inserted their gross, slug-like bodies into people's brains, and made them into slaves — Controllers. That is true.

Controllers are everywhere. My town. Your town. Everywhere.

They can be anyone. The policeman on the corner. The teacher in your school. Your best friend. Your mother or father. Your brother.

I know. Because my brother Tom is one of them.

Tom is a Controller. A slave to the Yeerk in his head. If he knew who I really was — *what* I really was — he would have me killed. Or turned into a Controller, like him.

That's what my world is like now. A world where the enemy is everywhere. Even sitting across from me at the breakfast table on a Saturday morning, which is when this part of the story begins.

"Hey, midget, what's up?" Tom asked as I sat down. That's one of the things he calls me. Actually I'm kind of big for my age. Almost as big as Tom. But it's a joke we've had for years. You know how it is.

"Not much," I said. "What's up with you?"

"Oh, I'm going to a meeting."

"The Sharing?" I asked, trying to sound casual. The Sharing is this group that tries to pretend that it's some kind of combined Boy Scouts and Girl Scouts. It's really a front organization for Controllers. The leadership council of The Sharing is made up of high-ranking Controllers.

"Yeah. We're doing some clean-up in the

park. You know, do our part for the community and all. Then we're having a barbecue afterwards." He gave me a serious look. "You really should join, you know. We'd get to spend more time together."

I felt a wave of sickness. I tried not to show it. It wasn't Tom talking. It was the Yeerk in his head. The Yeerk who wanted to take my body and use it as a host for one of his fellow slugs.

As I sat there across the table from him, I was trying to decide something. I was trying to decide whether I would ever have to destroy him. Destroy my brother, who was not my brother. Not any more.

"Maybe I will join some day," I said. *Like when hell freezes over,* I added silently. I poured myself some cereal and milk. "So you'll be out for a while?"

"All morning. Mum and Dad are out playing tennis, you'll have the house to yourself. Throw a party."

"Uh-huh," I said, and spooned up some cereal.

It was hard not to just yell at him. To let him know that I knew all about him. What he was. What he was doing.

At least, *some* of what he was doing. I had been spying on my brother. He was rising fast in the leadership of The Sharing. He was a very

loyal Controller. The Yeerk in his head had been promoted.

And he was involved in some new plan. A very big new plan.

A plan I had to stop. Even if . . .

"Well, take it easy, midget," Tom said, sounding just like he'd always sounded.

"You, too."

I waited till Tom was gone. I was alone. It was time.

I went through the house, room by room, making sure no one was there. Then I got the little matchbox I'd hidden in my desk drawer. I could hear a scrabbling noise coming from inside. I slid the matchbox open.

I shuddered.

It was a nice, big cockroach. Brown and glossy and about two centimetres long.

Its antennae waved eagerly. The roach tried to force its way out of the box, but I held my hand over it.

I could feel the roach antennae tickling the bottom of my palm. It was pushing, trying to get away.

I focused on the roach. Thought about it. Pictured it.

The roach stopped moving and lay still. Not dead, just quiet. The way animals always get when you "acquire" them.

I slid two fingers into the box to get a better contact with the roach. It felt hard and dry. I shuddered.

I absorbed the cockroach's DNA pattern. It was becoming part of me. The DNA — the genetic pattern — of many animals was a part of me now. Tiger. Dolphin. Flea. Falcon. Trout. Green anole lizard.

I have the power to morph. To become any animal that I can touch. The power was given to us, to me and my friends, by an Andalite prince moments before he was murdered by the Yeerks.

I have flown through the sky on my own outstretched wings at more than a hundred and sixty kilometres an hour. I have been a dolphin locked in deadly battle with sharks. I have felt the awesome power of the tiger, and experienced the terrible loss of self, the emptiness and horror of becoming an ant.

It was the gift of the dying Andalite. A powerful weapon for us to use in resisting the Yeerks.

It was also a dangerous, deadly curse. Like any weapon, I guess.

And now I was preparing to become a cockroach. It would be the ideal way to infiltrate The Sharing's new headquarters building. The Sharing's leadership meeting was in a couple of days. I wanted to be there. But the Yeerks had grown cautious lately.

They knew we were out here. They believed, wrongly, that we were a group of Andalite warriors, but they knew that morph-capable enemies were hunting them. Opposing them. Hurting them.

Sometimes hurting them very badly.

Tom. My brother. Could I destroy my own brother?

"You don't have to make that decision yet," I said aloud. "All you have to do now is try out this roach morph."

All I had to do now was become a cockroach.

Chapter 2

Cockroaches are not my favourite animals. But I knew a cockroach would be ideal for penetrating a guarded building. Roaches can go anywhere.

You may have noticed that fact.

I put my dog, Homer, out in the yard. I closed the curtains in my bedroom, making it as dark as possible.

"Oh, man, the things I do with my spare time," I muttered. I thought of calling Marco and asking him to come over. Marco is my best friend. He's the one who actually came up with the word "Animorph".

"No," I said. "Do this yourself."

The others were all tired. We'd had a rough time lately. Too many close calls. We needed a

rest. Time to deal with normal stuff, like school. Our grades had been suffering since we'd become Animorphs.

Besides, this had to be my decision. Tom was *my* brother.

I took a deep breath. I braced myself. I took another deep breath.

"OK, Jake," I said. "Let's do it."

The first mistake I made was standing in front of a full-length mirror.

It was dark in the room, but there was still enough light for me to see the changes.

Big mistake. Morphing is never pretty. It is always unpredictable. In fact, if you saw it happening and didn't know what was going on, you'd end up screaming for about two weeks straight.

The first feeling was of shrinking. It's exactly like falling. Like you're falling forever. I watched myself shrink in the mirror. It didn't look as bad in the mirror as it *felt*.

But what really did look bad was my skin as it began to be covered by an armour plate of brown cockroach shell.

"Aahhh!" I yelped in surprise.

My fingers melted together and formed a single, many-jointed bug leg. Antennae jumped out of my forehead. They seemed to stick out forever, then curl back, like they were being blown by a wind.

My waist was squeezed, and the lower part of my body swelled, forming a swollen insect abdomen. Swollen and brownish yellow with ripples, sort of like the Michelin man.

Then, when I was about half a metre tall, I felt the last of my bones dissolve. I could actually *hear* it happening. My spine had been grinding as it shrank. Then, suddenly, I heard a squishy sound, as all my internal organs lost their bone support.

My skull melted away. It was the last sound I heard clearly, as my ears and human sense of hearing faded.

I was a bag of loose guts. Almost deaf. Half-blind, as my human eyes shrank and the lenses became distorted.

My exoskeleton got harder and stiffer and stronger. My wings, glossy and crisp, covered my back. They overlapped at the edges, like the metal plates of a suit of armour.

Extra legs suddenly sprouted from my chest. Only it wasn't exactly a chest any more. I was a stunted, fifteen centimetre long bug, with a few disintegrating strands of brown hair and shrunken, but still somewhat human, eyes.

Not attractive. Not even slightly.

Then I lost my eyes. It took a second to even realize that I could still see. Then, oh yes! Yes, I could see. But not the way I saw with human eyes.

A weird, wavy mountain seemed to wrap all around me — my clothes. They looked different, blue and green and grey. Kind of. It's hard to describe, exactly. I couldn't see very far, just a few metres. And what I could see was shattered into dozens of little images. I saw little bits of vast fibrous walls — my socks. And dark tunnels made of thick slabs of what could have almost been wavy, corrugated concrete — the legs of my jeans.

The fibres of the carpet looked grey-green to me, and as big as ropes. My hairy, jointed roach legs would catch in the fibres as I tried to move.

I felt the roach brain surfacing. I'd been through it before. It's different each time, depending on the animal.

Sometimes it's a bunch of raw energy and fear that takes over your own mind so you think you're going crazy.

But not the roach brain. I didn't feel great hunger. I didn't feel great fear. The roach was . . . calm. Confident. Unworried.

I laughed. I mean, in my head I laughed, because I no longer had a mouth or a throat or anything at all that would make a laugh.

I was so tensed up, expecting the cockroach to be a bundle of energy and fear. But mostly it just felt like resting.

The roach brain wanted to take a nap.

Cool, I thought. It's gross. It's disgusting. Marco and the others will hate the idea, but when I tell them how easy it is to handle —

VIBRATION!

Get ready. Get ready. What was it? Get ready.

LIGHT! LIGHT! LIGHT!

Chapter 3

RUN! Run from the LIGHT!

Imagine being in one of those race cars at the Indianapolis 500.

Now imagine that instead of sitting in one, you are strapped face down *underneath* one. Your nose is about two millimetres from the road and you're going three hundred kilometres an hour.

That's what it was like when I ran. My roach legs powered like something from a Roadrunner cartoon. I blew out from under the folds of my own clothing. I blew across that carpet. I was rocket-propelled.

Someone had put the light on in my room. And when that light came on, my roach brain stopped being calm and relaxed.

Zoooom! Five kilometres an hour. That's very fast when you're only three centimetres long.

Vibration . . . vibration . . . vibration . . .

Heavy steps rattled the floor. They vibrated up through my legs. My tiny roach brain knew what they meant. Something very, very big was walking around.

Chasing me! RUN!

Zoom! across the carpet. Suddenly, a wall!

Up? Left? Right? Which way?

Vibration . . . vibration . . . vibration . . .

Wait! A crack. It wasn't much of a crack. Just enough space to slip a coin through. No way I could fit.

Or could I?

My underside scraped the floor. My hard brown wing cover scraped the bottom of the skirting-board. But I barely had to slow down.

I was in the wall! Hah! The big things that rattled the floor would never catch me now. I was safe here. A nail as thick as a tree trunk stuck up from the wood. I went around it.

On either side of me I saw bright, straight lines of light that seemed to go on forever. They were the cracks beneath the skirting-boards. To one side a thick, shiny slab with irregular edges intruded into the wall — the edge of the kitchen linoleum.

High above I could see other bright lights,

more circular and dimmer. These were the holes where pipes entered the wall.

AHHHH!

Something moving! Close by. Oh, gross! A cockroach!

Get a grip, Jake! I told myself. *You're* a cockroach, too! But still, you just don't want to be face-to-face with a roach as big as you are. I mean, he was right at eye level. The other roach's antennae felt me, sweeping over me, tangling briefly with my antennae.

We said "hi." At least, we said the roach version of "hi." Which wasn't really "hello". It was more like, "Oh, you're a roach, too."

Now, in the darkness inside the wall, I felt calmer. The electric fear was gone. The suddenness of the light had been the problem. That and the vibration.

I could still feel the vibrations, but they were different now. Further away.

OK, I'd had enough of being a roach. It was time to get to some safe place, demorph and find out who had been in my room.

Why was someone in my room? A few minutes earlier, and they would have caught me in mid-morph. Stupid of me. Stupid, stupid.

Where could I go to demorph? The garage? Yes, the garage. There weren't any mirrors, and I sure didn't want to watch myself morph again.

Through the kitchen, out under the back door; that was the way.

I went to the bright crack ahead of me, the kitchen. I scampered up on the ledge of linoleum. I stuck my head and antennae out beneath the skirting-board. The vibrations were all far away. In some other room.

I emerged from the crack. Over my head was an incredibly high canyon. It went up and up, far higher than I could see. Two parallel walls, just a few body lengths apart. Of course. The fridge. I was behind the fridge. One side of the "canyon" was the kitchen wall, the other side was the back of the fridge.

Someone really should sweep back here. There were dust balls the size of couches.

But no problem. I was getting the hang of it now. Follow the skirting-board. To the next wall. Turn right, and then there would be the door.

No problem. I was in charge.

Some big barn-like structure was ahead of me. It looked like one of those old-fashioned covered bridges.

Huh. Probably an old matchbox.

I went in, trotting along on my six jointed legs.

Wait. I wasn't moving any more.

What the . . . ?

I tried to run.

I was stuck!

I tried again. One leg was free, but the others were frozen in place. What was . . . I felt around with my antennae.

Now my antennae were stuck!

I couldn't move. I couldn't move at all!

I was trapped!

Chapter 4

"So?" Rachel demanded. "What was it? How did you get trapped?"

"I'll bet I know," Marco said, grinning sardonically, which is the only way he knows how to grin. "Jake checked in, but he couldn't check out."

I nodded. "Roach Motel. I walked into a stupid Roach Motel. I ran right on to the sticky paper and, man, I could not move. Very frustrating."

"You know, you could do commercials for the Roach Motel company," Marco suggested. "Take it from me, Roach Boy, these things really work."

It was later in the day, and we were in Cassie's barn. Rachel, Marco, Tobias, Cassie and me. As usual, the place was filled with wire

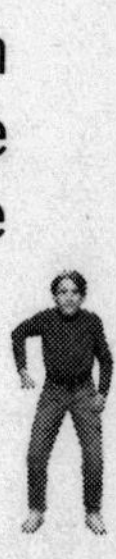

cages, and the cages were filled with animals. Rabbits, foxes, baby deer, eagles, opossums, mourning doves, all of them injured or sick. Some of them feisty and ready to be released.

We were lounging around on bales of hay and piles of feed sacks. All except Tobias, who was up in the rafters high overhead, and Cassie, who was feeding some of the animals.

Everyone seemed to think my roach experiment was funny.

Except for Cassie. Cassie was the only one not smiling. She was giving me a very disapproving look. "Jake, you of all people should know better."

She was right. I knew she was right. But that just made me stubborn.

"Look, I was just trying out the morph to see if it would be good for us to use."

Cassie totally did not buy my argument. She put down the bucket she was carrying. She took off her heavy work gloves. She came over and stood about a metre from me. Then she stuck her finger in my face.

"Uh-oh," Marco said in a loud whisper. "Jake's in trouble."

"Big time," Rachel agreed.

"Jake," Cassie said, "don't *ever* do that again. Now, you are sort of the one in charge, but I am *telling* you, don't *ever* do that again.

Don't ever try some new morph without one of us there. Do you understand?"

"Cassie, I was just —"

"Uh-uh. No. Don't tell me what you were *just*. Don't ever do that again."

<Um, Jake? I think this is the point where you just say 'yes, ma'am,'> Tobias said, in the thought-speak that comes with being in a morph.

I hung my head. "OK, Cassie. Sorry."

Rachel whistled appreciatively. "It's a new, tougher Cassie. I approve."

"I remember when she used to be so sweet," Marco said. "I didn't know her voice could even sound like that. Plus, look! She now comes with a Kung Fu grip."

Cassie ignored them. Instead she gave me a private look, just between the two of us. I knew what the look meant. It meant *I care about you. Don't be dumb.*

And the look I sent her meant *I know. I care about you, too.*

OK, I realize it sounds corny. But give me a break. We'd been through a lot, Cassie and I. And all of us. We'd grown pretty close.

To me, Cassie is an amazing person. For one thing, she handles all kinds of responsibility. Her barn is actually the Wildlife Rehabilitation Clinic. Her parents are both vets and her dad

runs the clinic as a way to help injured wild animals. Everything from seagulls to skunks. And Cassie helps with all the work, except for doing surgery. But I'll bet she could do that, too.

As for how she looks, well, she's very pretty. Kind of short. She only comes up to my chin, but then, I'm fairly tall. But she's not one of those wimpy-looking short girls, you know? Not all prissy. She's strong-looking. Mostly, when I picture Cassie, I think of her wearing overalls and boots because of working in the barn so much.

I guess most guys would say Rachel is prettier. Personally, I don't think of her that way because she's my cousin. But Rachel does look like some kind of blonde supermodel.

Not that Rachel acts like Ms Fashion. Just the opposite. If there's danger, Rachel is right there. Usually a few steps ahead of anyone else.

Marco says Rachel's enjoying it all. That she's actually glad about all that's happened in our lives since that night when we saw the Andalites' damaged spaceship land in the construction site. Marco refers to Rachel as *Xena, Warrior Princess.*

But that's Marco. For him, everything is a joke. Except for his family. Or what's left of it.

Marco is small, with dark eyes and dark, long brown hair. Cassie says a lot of the girls at school think he's cute. I wouldn't know.

Most of the time Marco and I totally do not get along. He says I'm too serious. Personally, I think he's just a little too immature sometimes.

We disagree about everything. He actually tries to tell me that college hoops are better than the NBA. Yeah, right! Please. What are you going to do with a guy like that?

We get on each other's nerves a lot of the time.

We're also best friends and have been since we were babies. I would do almost anything for Marco, and he would do the same for me. Of course, he'd complain the whole time. Oh, man, can that guy complain when he wants to.

The last member of our original group is Tobias. Tobias used to be this kind of sweet guy with wild blond hair. A dreamy sort of person with a really terrible home life.

Used to be.

I glanced up at him. He was perched on a rafter overhead. He was preening his wing feathers, carefully combing them out with his beak.

It's an amazing beak. It has a wicked, cruel-looking hook at the end — the better to tear open the mice and rats and other small animals he eats.

Tobias is a red-tailed hawk. I guess maybe he will always be a red-tailed hawk.

See, there's one problem with morphing. A time limit of two hours. If you stay in morph more than two hours, you stay for ever.

Which is why Rachel asked me, "So? What's the rest of the story? How did you get out of the Roach Motel before the time was up? I notice you are human again."

"More or less," Marco added.

I shrugged. "Well, I sat there for a while, trying to squirm out, but it didn't work. I was stuck good. But it was OK, because as I sat there I realized I could start to make sense of some of the vibrations I was hearing. Some of it was sound. People speaking."

"What people?" Marco asked.

"My parents. My dad twisted his ankle playing tennis, which is why they'd come home early. They were the ones who'd gone into my room, looking for the Ace bandage I have in my drawer. They were the ones who'd turned on the light. Anyway, what could I do? I wasn't about to get stuck in roach morph. And I could tell my parents were up in their bedroom. So I demorphed."

<Wait. Weren't you behind the fridge?> Tobias asked in thought-speak.

"Yeah. And it was very tight. But as I grew, I could push the fridge out a centimetre at a time. Still, I thought I was going to suffocate back there. And then, just as I was getting human again, my mum walks in."

That made them all lean forward.

"What?" Cassie demanded. "Your mum? What did she *see*? What did she *say*?"

"Well, all she could see was my head. It was normal, fortunately. And what she asked me was, 'Jake? Why are you back there? And while we're at it, why do you have the top of a Roach Motel stuck in your hair?'"

Everyone got a good laugh out of that image.

Marco was the first to stop laughing. He was looking at me kind of sideways. The way he does when he thinks I'm hiding something.

"Very funny and all, Jake," Marco said. "But you haven't told us why you were morphing a roach. And don't give me that 'I was just trying it out' routine."

I stopped laughing. Sooner or later I would have to tell them. I would have to tell them everything.

"OK. Look, I've learned something. For one thing, Tom is getting more important to the Yeerks. I think now he's just below Chapman as a Controller."

Rachel gave a low whistle.

Chapman is our assistant principal at school. He is also the most important Controller we know about.

"Tom is careful about not letting my parents or me overhear anything suspicious," I said. "But he does make phone calls using our phone sometimes. I've been checking the automatic redial when he's done. So I know some of the people he's calling."

Marco laughed. "Cool. Jake the superspy. Nice trick."

<And who is Tom calling?> Tobias asked.

"Doctors. Five different doctors. I looked them up in the phone book. They all practise at the same hospital. The same wing of the hospital, at something called the Berman Clinic. Berman is one of the doctors Tom calls."

It took a few minutes for the facts to sink in.

"Wait a minute," Rachel said. "Are you saying the Yeerks are running that hospital? Or at least a part of that hospital? Why would they want a hospital?"

I hesitated before answering. I wasn't sure my guess was right. Maybe I was just being paranoid. But Marco, who could teach a class in paranoia, had already figured it out, of course.

"Oh, man. They're going to use the hospital to infest host bodies. You check in to have your tonsils out or to have a cast put on your broken arm. You check out as a Controller."

Chapter 5

Tom came home late that evening. He smelled like wood smoke and barbecue sauce.

My mum and dad and I were already at the table, eating dinner. My dad had his injured ankle resting on a stool. We were having broiled chicken and potatoes and veggies.

As he walked in through the kitchen door, my mum said, "Tom, how was the big clean-up? They showed some of it on the news."

Tom came into the dining room and took a chair across from me. "It was OK. We filled two dump-bins full of rubbish and dead branches and stuff. Hey, what happened to your leg, old man?"

My dad winced. "I tried for a shot I shouldn't have tried for. Twisted it."

"Did you have enough to eat?" my mum asked Tom.

Tom patted his stomach. "Burgers and hot-dogs and chicken. Not as good as your chicken, of course."

"Actually, your father cooked. He cooked by calling Gourmet Express and having it delivered."

"But I did microwave the sauce," my dad said. "That counts as cooking."

Tom winked at my dad. "Well, the stuff at the barbecue had to be better than dad's chicken. Good thing I ate there."

"Just for that you get no dessert," my dad said. "And it's cheesecake. From Santorini's."

"Oooh, Santorini's?" Tom groaned. "I take it back. I apologize. I grovel. I beg. I love Santorini's."

Homer came in, sensing it was time for table scraps. "Hey, Homer," Tom said. He scratched him behind the ears and Homer got his happy-moron look, the look where his eyes glaze over and his tongue lolls out of his mouth.

A totally normal scene. Around a totally normal dinner table. No one would ever have guessed the truth. In my brother's head was an alien. A creature from another planet.

I asked Ax about how it works. Ax is the Andalite we rescued from the bottom of the ocean. He's one of us now, I guess.

Anyway, I asked Ax about how the Yeerk slug lives in a person's head. He'd explained it to me. How they can flatten their slug-like bodies. How they can sink between the crevices and cracks of a person's brain. How they melt like a liquid into every available space. How they wrap their bodies around a brain and attach their own neurons to human neurons.

Tom must have noticed me staring at him.

"What's your malfunction?"

I snapped out of my daze. "What? Oh, nothing. I was just thinking of something."

"You were staring at me. You were staring at my forehead."

I forced a laugh. My mind raced to think of a joke. "Really? I thought I was just staring blankly into empty space. But then again, empty space, your head. What's the difference?"

It worked. Tom snatched up a dinner roll and chucked it at me. I caught it in mid-air a split second before it would have hit my face.

For a moment we just glared at each other.

"Don't throw food," my dad said. "It's undignified."

"It's OK," I said. "Tom's not fast enough to hit me any more. He's slowed down. Lost his touch."

Tom raised an eyebrow. "Don't push it, midget."

I smiled. It was a fake smile, but it was the best I could do. "You used to be faster when you were still on the basketball team. I guess hanging out at The Sharing all the time, eating barbecue and potato salad, must have slowed your reflexes."

You know, in the old days, Tom would not have put up with that. He would not have let me challenge him and get away with it. He would have had me in a headlock and given me a massive noogie till I begged for mercy.

But now he just gave me a cold, uncertain smile.

Maybe it was because he had changed. Maybe it was because I had changed. The silence stretched between us for a few minutes, and my parents, feeling uncomfortable, made small talk.

"I have homework to do," I said at last. "May I be excused?"

"Come back down for cheesecake later," my mum said.

Tom caught up with me on the stairs. "I don't know why you're so against The Sharing," he said. "A lot of the kids in your school have joined."

"I guess I just don't like to join things."

"Yeah? Well, don't dump on what you don't understand. What were you doing that was so important today? While I was out cleaning up the park?"

I stopped and turned to face him. I was one step higher than he was. We were eye to eye. "Me? I wasn't doing much of anything. Hanging out with Marco."

"Your loss," he said. "There are things that are cooler than hanging out with Marco. Cooler than being on some bogus team. Important things. You could be a part of something . . . bigger. You could be part of something great, not just another nothing kid."

He gave me a look. Like he could tell me incredible things. Like he could open up a whole new world for me.

I could be part of something bigger. Something important.

I knew that kind of stuff worked on some people. That was the first step towards becoming a voluntary host. That was how The Sharing started you out: talk of bigger, more glorious, more interesting things that you could be part of.

Part of.

"Thanks, Tom," I said. "But I don't want to be a *part*. I guess I'd rather just be one person. On my own. One little nothing kid."

For a split second after I said that, he let the mask slip. For just a moment I saw an expression

of pure arrogance and contempt. Yeerk arrogance. Yeerk contempt.

The look said "We will have you, sooner or later. You and all the rest of your weak race."

Then it was gone, and Tom was shrugging like it was all no big deal.

I went to my room. I did some homework. Later, I went back downstairs and ate cheesecake along with my folks and my brother. One big happy family watching TV and pigging out.

That night, I had the dream.

A dream that had begun to appear almost every night.

Chapter 6

"I can't believe we are actually going to practise a morph," Marco said. "We never practise. We just do it, and when it's a huge disaster we try and deal with it then."

"We need the practice," I pointed out. "We're going in as spies. We're going to this thing to try and hear what they are saying. And it takes a while to learn how to use the cockroach's senses to understand sound."

"This would be a great horror movie. Or at least a book," Marco said. "*Roachman*."

We were in Marco's new apartment. It was the first time we'd ever used it. Probably because now that Marco's dad was back at work, they had moved to a better place. I guess Marco used to

be embarrassed over his old place.

In fact, his dad was out, working late at his new job. I hoped the job would last. Marco had been carrying a big load of family problems for a long time.

"Is it possible to die of total willies?" Cassie asked. "I mean, do you think we could some day just gross ourselves right out of existence? I didn't even like touching a cockroach. How am I going to stand becoming one?"

"Just don't be near a mirror," I suggested. "And don't look at each other while you're morphing."

<Are these creatures frightening to humans?> Ax wondered.

It's amazing how quickly we'd all become used to the fact that this guy from another planet was with us. I barely even thought about the fact that an Andalite was standing there, looking like a cross between a blue deer, a mouthless human, a goat with eyes on the ends of his horns, and a scorpion.

The scorpion part is the Andalite's tail. It has a curved, scythe blade on the end. The Andalites can whip that tail forward so fast you don't even see it move.

I sat on the edge of Marco's bed. Tobias perched just inside the window, looking fierce and angry — although, of course, he wasn't.

Speaking of odd things I was getting used to. I mean, I was there with an alien, my cousin, my best friend, and Cassie, and they were all getting ready to become roaches.

Except for Tobias.

And the weirdest thing of all was that it didn't seem weird any more.

I watched as they all began to morph. I looked away when it began to get disgusting. When I looked again, there were four cockroaches on the carpet.

<OK,> Marco thought-spoke to me. <We're bugs. Let's get this over with, because I have to tell you — I have a major urge to step on myself.>

"OK," I said. "Can you guys hear me?"

<Go ahead. We're ready. Say something,> Marco thought-spoke. I couldn't tell which roach was him. All roaches look alike.

"Hello," I said loudly.

<Wait. I felt something,> Cassie said.

"Tobias, tell them that was me."

<That was Jake,> Tobias translated into thought-speak. <He said 'hello.'>

<OK, Jake. Do it again. Say 'hello' again,> Marco instructed.

"Hello."

<Yeah, I felt some vibrations there,> Rachel confirmed.

"Hello."

<That sounded like hello,> Cassie said.

<Jake?> Marco said. <Say 'I'm a huge dork.' I'll see if I can understand it.>

"You're a huge dork."

<Very funny,> Marco said. <I couldn't actually hear what you said. But I know you.>

We spent about an hour with Marco, Cassie, Rachel and Ax learning to translate vibration into human speech. They were repeating the learning I'd done while I was stuck in a Roach Motel behind my fridge.

When they demorphed I looked away again. My dreams had been weird enough lately. I didn't need any help having nightmares.

Cassie is the best morpher in our group, even better than Ax — who's an Andalite, after all. Usually she can kind of control the process a little. Once, when we were morphing birds, she managed to turn totally human except for keeping huge bird wings for a few seconds.

It was really cool.

But even Cassie couldn't do anything to make a cockroach morph attractive.

It was disgusting. Flat-out disgusting.

<You have such wonderful animals on this planet,> Ax said when he had returned to his normal form. Not that his normal form looked very normal, standing there in Marco's bedroom.

"Cockroaches are not wonderful," Rachel said, shuddering a little. "I mean, I'm sorry, but I don't like those bodies."

"They're easy to handle, though," Marco said. "Not like ants."

We all exchanged a look. We'd had a very bad experience with ants. That was one morph no one was going to be repeating.

"You know, guys, this mission doesn't really require all of us to go," I said.

"Look, I just said roaches are disgusting," Rachel protested. "I didn't say I didn't want to do it. We need to know what's going on with that hospital. The best way to do that is to crash this leadership meeting of The Sharing. And the best way to do that is with roach morphs. End of discussion."

She looked around belligerently, as if she was daring anyone to disagree.

"Yeah, but I can do it alone," I said.

"What's going on with you?" Rachel asked. "You know we're the Five Musketeers. One for all, and all for one. Six Musketeers now," she corrected, looking at Ax.

<What are Musketeers?> Ax asked.

No one answered him. They were all just looking at me like I'd done something wrong.

"Normally, I'd be all for staying out of trouble," Marco said. "But I'm just curious about

why you're acting this way."

"It makes sense. One of us can go it alone."

"Are you worried about Tom getting hurt?" Cassie asked.

Count on Cassie to figure it out. I looked down at the ground. "Look, he is my brother. You guys are my friends. What if we get into it and it comes down to a fight?"

Marco raised his eyebrows thoughtfully. He understood. "We don't hurt Tom, that's the first thing."

"It's not that simple," I said. "He's involved in this big time. He's one of *them*. And he would . . . look, he would kill any of us."

I hated having to say that. But it was true.

<Not Tom,> Tobias said. <The thing that lives in his head. Never Tom.>

I sighed. "I had this dream." I almost stopped talking right there, because I felt like a fool bringing it up. "I know this is stupid. I know dreams don't mean anything. But I've had this dream a couple of times."

"So? Tell us," Rachel prodded.

"OK, but don't laugh. In the dream I'm in my tiger morph. And I'm stalking Tom. Following him. On his trail. I'm feeling the tiger's eagerness. You know, that predator feeling. The hunger. The desire to kill."

Tobias turned his head away. I knew why.

Tobias was a predator now. He felt that eagerness, that killing desire, every day. It still bothered him, I guess. He had always been such a gentle guy. Back when he was fully human.

"Anyway, in the dream, I'm hunting my own brother. Only, when I get close . . . he turns around. And it isn't Tom any more. It's . . ." I stopped myself before I finished the sentence. I'd already said too much.

"I just don't want anything to happen to Tom," I said lamely. "It's not just about what might happen if there's a fight. It's . . . Look, I think Tom is important to this whole hospital plan somehow. I think maybe he's in charge. If we manage to stop this thing, who knows what they'll do to Tom? I mean, maybe Visser Three just kills Tom's Yeerk. But we've all seen Visser Three in action. He likes to make examples out of anyone who fails him. He could kill Tom."

Rachel whistled softly. "If we succeed, Tom fails. If he fails, Visser Three may kill him."

"That's about the way it is, yeah," I said.

"So, what do we do?" Marco asked.

"We forget this mission," Cassie suggested.

"And leave the Yeerks in control of a hospital? A little factory for making Controllers?" I countered. "Why? Because my brother may be hurt?"

"Yes," Cassie said simply.

I hesitated. I wanted to agree. But how could I justify backing off for selfish reasons?

"We don't have to make a final decision now," Marco said. "We can go in. Learn what they're up to. Decide then what to do about it."

I met Marco's gaze. I wondered what he was thinking about me. Only Marco and I know about his mother. To everyone else, she's dead. Only the two of us know that she's really a Controller. That her body is the host body of Visser One.

Marco, of all people, understood what I was dealing with. He had given me a way out of deciding.

"Yeah," I said, nodding at my friend. "Marco's right. This is just a spy mission. There's plenty of time to decide what to do, when we know more about what they are up to."

I should have felt relieved.

I didn't.

Chapter 7

"How long do you think this will take?" Rachel asked. She checked her watch. "I set the video for two of my favourite shows, but I forgot to tape the movie of the week."

"I'm taping it in case you miss it," Cassie said.

It was dark out, but not very late. The moon was up, but hidden by the clouds. We were walking along the street, doing our best to look like a normal bunch of kids just hanging out.

Normal.

<This sucks,> Tobias said from high above. <I'm half-blind at night. Especially without moonlight. I should have got myself stuck in an owl body. Owls are so cool. Aside from the fact that some of them try to kill and eat falcons.>

"How can you ever run in these bodies?" Ax wondered. "Two legs? It is absurd. Surd. Ubsurd. Ubzerd. Not even a tail to help you stay up."

Ax was in his human morph. It's a combination of DNA from me, Marco, Rachel and Cassie. The result is kind of like looking at all of us at once, but in one body. It's really weird.

Ax had almost got used to having a mouth when he was in his human morph. Almost. He still had a tendency to want to play with sounds, repeating them. Plus, the boy was dangerous when he got around food. The sense of taste was just overwhelming for him.

"You know, Ax, now that you mention it . . ." Marco started gyrating wildly, like a guy out of control. "I only have two legs! I'm falling . . . falling!"

"See? I knew it must happen sometimes," Ax said, adding, "Happen. Hap. Hap. Pun."

I wasn't sure if Ax knew Marco was being funny or not. Ax might have a very dry sense of humour. Or he might have no sense of humour at all. I hadn't figured it out yet.

"There's the place," I said. It was up ahead, at the end of the block.

It was a residential neighbourhood, with older houses and a few kind of low-budget shops mixed in. You know, thrift shops and car parts places and small restaurants.

Our target was a single-storey, whitewashed building. There was only one door, and the windows were high up, narrow and long. They were blocked off so that no one could see inside. There was a small car park with about a dozen cars in it.

Over the door was a sign: "The Sharing. Building a Better Life."

"Yeah, right," Marco sneered. "A better life for slugs from outer space. You notice the guy standing by the door? He looks like he's ready for trouble."

A very large man stood by the door, muscular arms folded over his chest. But we'd expected that. Marco and Rachel and I had scoped the place out ahead of time.

"OK, we cut down this alley," I said. "That building down there is abandoned. The basement is empty and unlocked. That's where we morph."

The basement was dark and depressing and smelled of mildew. I guess it used to be part of a restaurant. There were still some old tables strewn around. There were also a lot of old beer bottles and bits of rubbish.

"Wonderful," Rachel said in a whisper. "This whole Animorph lifestyle is so glamorous."

Tobias fluttered in through the open door. Then we heard a thump.

<Ow! Man, who put a pillar there? Banged my right wing.>

"Great. This is the guy who's supposed to be looking out for us," Marco grumbled.

Ax had instantly begun to morph back to his Andalite body. It is not possible to go straight from one morph to another. Just like we have to return to human form between morphs, he had to resume Andalite form.

"Come on, let's do this and get it over with," Rachel said. "I'm going to be a roach in a filthy basement. My mother would be so proud if she knew."

"Wait," Cassie said. "We agree on how this works, right? We're not looking for a fight. This is a spy mission. No one do anything dramatic, like morph into an elephant and go on a stomping spree."

Cassie was looking at Rachel. Rachel has an elephant morph. She's very fond of it.

Rachel laughed. "Absolutely. Spy time. Stealth is my middle name."

"OK." I was a little embarrassed that Cassie had brought it up. She was trying to remind everyone that Tom was one of the Controllers in that meeting. Trying to remind everyone that we were just there for information.

"Let's morph already," Rachel said. "Come on. I'll miss the movie."

"Five little roaches. We'll be right at home in this dump," Marco said as he began the transformation. "You will keep the rats from eating us, won't you, Tobias?"

<Hey, I may not see that well in the dark, but I can still catch a rat, light or no light. I am the rat-killer of the universe.>

"Ax? You ready?"

<Yes, Prince Jake. I am fully Andalite and ready to become your roach.>

A few moments later, we were five cockroaches amid the scattered rubbish on the bare concrete floor.

<Wow. That is one big beer can,> Marco said.

A blue and white can towered over us, curving away into the sky.

<Let's, um, scurry,> I said. <Ax? You keep track of the time.>

We took off, a little knot of fast-moving roaches, all running in the same direction.

<You know, if this wasn't so gross, it would be kind of cool,> Rachel said. <Stairs! All right. A little vertical rock climbing.>

Tiny pincers on the end of my six legs grabbed the small protrusions of concrete and wedged into invisible cracks. It all happened so fast and so automatically that I could run straight up the cement step, almost as fast as I could move horizontally.

Up the riser. Over the edge. *Zoom,* to the next riser. Up. Over. Across. To the top of the four stairs.

<You know, you guys still give me the willies,> Tobias said. <You should see yourselves. The urge to step on you is pretty strong — if I had shoes. I never did like roaches.>

<This from a guy who disembowels live mice for lunch,> Marco said.

<Don't knock it if you haven't tried it,> Tobias shot back.

In some corner of my mind I noted the fact that Tobias seemed more and more at peace with his weird life — half-bird, half-human.

But mostly my mind was on the job at hand. We had reached the threshold. We scampered across it and out into the alley.

The alley was a mix of gravel and cracked, torn-up tarmac. The tarmac was like running across hard oatmeal, all bumpy and uneven. The gravel was more difficult. The pieces of rock were as big as we were, and even with our six clever legs, there was a lot of stumbling and slipping.

<I'm going airborne,> Tobias said. <You're out on the pavement. Turn left. There's better light out here so I'll be able to watch you from the top of the telephone pole.>

<OK, we'd better spread out. Don't forget, these are Controllers. Yeerks. They believe there

is a group of Andalite warriors running around loose. In other words, they'll be on the lookout for morphs. So act like normal roaches.>

<You mean I should crawl inside an open box of cereal?> Marco asked. <I had that happen once. I almost ate the bug. Yuck.>

We fanned out, staying several centimetres apart as we moved towards the building. I stopped when I reached the whitewashed cinder block of the exterior wall.

<Crack!> Cassie called. <I found a big crack here. I'm going in.>

The rest of us waited. I felt obvious, just sitting there. Obvious and helpless. The big guy at the door could decide to step on me. I couldn't see him, but I knew he was there.

<This is good,> Cassie said from deep in the wall. <I think we can follow it all the way inside.>

One by one, we scurried to her location. I felt better when I was inside the crack. Until I thought about what would happen if I tried to demorph in such a tight spot.

I didn't even want to start thinking about that.

<We're going in, Tobias,> I called to him. <Get somewhere safe.>

<I'm cool,> he said. <Good luck.>

We were travelling single file, sideways, along the crack. It was like exploring a cave. There was

no light, but my antennae felt the way, picking up the scent of the others, reading the tiny air currents, sniffing for familiar aromas.

Then I saw a faint light that grew brighter as I advanced. Cassie was in the lead. <It worked. It goes all the way through. I'm inside.>

I sidled up beside her. I could see through the crack opening now. I could see brilliant light. And I could feel vibration.

The vibration of sound. Of speech.

I concentrated. It was impossible to tell much about the voice. Who it was. It seemed too high to be someone old.

Was it Tom?

I listened to the words.

". . . the day is here at last. It is time to strike the decisive blow in the invasion of Earth."

Chapter 8

<What is this, a Yeerk pep rally?> Marco wondered.

Cassie started giggling — well thought-speak giggling —, and pretty soon all of us, except Ax, were laughing silently. Although it was very nervous laughter.

<We need to get out of this crack,> I said. <Spread out a little. We look too obvious just sitting here, and we should try to see if we can identify some of these people. Move out. But wait! Not all at once!>

Too late. We were all scampering down the wall from the crack to the floor. To anyone watching it would have looked like "Invasion of the Roaches." Five roaches, moving all together,

is an easy thing to notice.

But I had forgotten one thing. Humans hate roaches. A human will spot a roach very quickly. But Yeerks couldn't care less. Even though these were all human-Controllers, they were with their fellow Yeerks now. They didn't have to keep up the "human" act.

No one stomped us. Although I waited for a big shoe to drop from the sky.

We separated a little, then headed along the edge of the wall, where bare concrete floor met painted cinder block walls.

<Hey, guys? Can you hear me? It's Tobias.>

<Just barely, but I can still understand you,> I called back. Thought-speak gets weaker over distances. Same as regular speech. Although walls and so on aren't a problem.

<There's a car pulling up outside here. A limo. And there are two other cars with it, full of very tough-looking dudes.>

<What are they doing?>

<Getting out, now. Like six guys. They have guns! I can see them under their coats. Now there's a guy getting out of the back of the limo.>

<Who is it? Or should I say, *what* is it?>

<He's a human. He staggered a little, walking towards the door. He looks like a normal guy, but all the others are acting very nervous. And . . . I

know this sounds dumb, but I get a bad feeling from this guy.>

Now I could hear the vibrations of many feet walking fast. <They're coming our way now, Tobias. Thanks for the warning.>

I tried to use my eyes, but they were hopeless at any kind of distance. All I could tell was that several men had arrived and were marching through the room.

"My brothers-in-arms," some loud, booming voice said, "I present to you, our leader. Visser Three."

There was a gasp from the group. There was a silent gasp from us, too.

Visser Three?

Visser Three had an Andalite body. He was the only Yeerk ever to obtain an Andalite body, with all its morphing power. But surely, Tobias would have mentioned seeing an Andalite getting out of a car.

"I see that some of you are surprised," a new voice said. "Surely you must know that I can morph a human, as well as any other body."

<Oh, man,> Marco said. <Visser Three can morph a human?>

<Certainly,> Ax said. <Just as I do. Humans are animals, after all. You have DNA.>

The voice we now knew as Visser Three spoke in a hard, curt tone. It was odd, hearing his

words. We had only heard him thought-speak before. Now he had a voice. And, if we could only see it, a human body. But he was too far away for our weak and distorted roach vision.

"This mission has two parts. One. We will use the front hospital to take involuntary hosts. I expect to be able to make two hundred new Controllers per Earth month. We will concentrate on police, broadcasters, writers, teachers, people in finance, and especially anyone in a position of political power."

There was a murmur of excitement from the assembled crowd.

<Just what we were afraid of,> I said.

<Unfortunately,> Marco agreed. <Man, two hundred new Controllers a month?>

"You have done well recruiting human doctors and nurses, so that we now control the hospital facility. But this brings me to the second part of the mission," Visser Three said. "Until now this secret was known only to me and a very small group."

The room was almost totally silent, listening, anticipating.

"The second part of my plan is even more important than the first. In a few days, the governor of this state will have some minor surgery performed. His secretary is one of us, and she has steered him to our facility. He will check in for the minor surgery. When he checks out . . . he will belong to us."

<No,> Rachel gasped.

<What does it mean? What is a *governor*? Is this some sort of prince?> Ax asked.

<Yeah. A prince. The governor controls the state police,> I said. <And the National Guard. And the schools.>

<It's worse than that,> Rachel said grimly. <Don't you guys ever pay attention to politics?>

<What are you talking about?>

<Don't you know? Our governor is getting ready to run for president next year. A year from now there could be a Controller in the White House.>

<A White House? What does all this mean?> Ax asked.

<It means that one of *them* could be the most powerful man in the most powerful nation on Earth,> I said.

<And that would be the ball game,> Marco said.

<Then . . . all would be lost?>

<Yeah, Ax. All would be lost.>

Chapter 9

<Let's bail. We've learned all we need to know,> I said.

<Back to the crack?> Cassie asked.

<Yeah. We know the way.>

I turned and headed back to the crack. It was only thirty centimetres or so away. In a few seconds we would all be safe.

I could not believe what I had heard. It was insane! If the Yeerks succeeded, we were toast, pure and simple. As long as it was a secretive war between us and Yeerks who did not want to be discovered, we could maybe stay alive. But if all the power of the state police were turned against us, too? The situation would be out of —

Suddenly, a strange vibration in the air above me.

DANGER!

RUN!

WHHHAAAMMMPP!

It was like someone had dropped an entire three-bedroom house just in front of me.

The impact was awesome. The wind it caused was like a small but intense hurricane. It whipped my antennae back.

<Someone almost stepped on me!> I yelled to the others. <Look out!>

"Visser! Forgive my interruption. But there are several small insects here!"

A general murmur from the crowd, then one voice saying, "Don't worry, they are only cockroaches. They are everywhere on this planet."

"Fool!" Visser Three exploded. "Do you think Andalites cannot morph creatures so small? Someone kill this fool for me."

BLAM! BLAM!

I felt the world spinning around me. Someone had been shot! Was it . . . Tom? Could it have been?

A new rush of air overhead. I could see something monstrously huge falling towards me, speeding down, ready to crush me.

I bolted.

WWHHHAAAMMMPP!

Millimetres from my tail.

"Kill those insects!" Visser Three screamed.

<Everyone for himself!> I yelled. <Spread out. Run! Get into cracks! Let the roach brains guide you!>

I took my own advice and relinquished control to the raw instincts and cunning of the tiny cockroach brain.

Say what you will about roaches. They're gross. They're disgusting. But man, when it comes to staying alive, that primitive roach brain knew its business.

WWHHAAAMPPP!

WWHHAAMMMPP!

<Aaaahhh!> Ax yelled.

<Ax! Are you okay?>

<Yes. Yes. Barely.>

Huge feet, each the size of a Greyhound bus, stamped the ground. But each time, the roach brain moved me in just the right way at just the right speed. They missed me by so little that I could feel the leather and rubber scrape my sides and tail as they impacted around me.

I made it to the corner of the wall and hugged in there as close as I could get.

<They're on me!> Cassie screamed. <I can't get away! Oh, man! I don't want to die like this!>

<Get to the wall! Get off the floor!>

I was blazing along at top speed as shoes

tried to kick into the corner. But all I needed was two millimetres and I could scrape past, uninjured.

SQQQUUUUEEEEEGGGEE.

A running shoe was being dragged along the corner, straight towards me. The soft rubber melded perfectly into the space. It would crush me!

I saw it coming, a black wall. A black locomotive rushing at me.

I jumped!

I landed on the shoe as it came near.

Whooosshhh! I was flying through the air on a magic carpet made of canvas. The man kicked. I lost my grip and went flying through the air.

<I'm clear! I'm clear!> Cassie called. <I've found another crack!>

I felt like I was going supersonic. Like a jet, tumbling out of control through the air.

Wait! I had wings!

Too late.

Fwappp! I hit the wall. It should have killed me. It would have killed me if I had been a human. But I weighed only a few grammes. The impact was hard, but not enough to hurt me.

I fell to the floor.

A tent of some sort — grey, black . . . a newspaper! It was a crumpled piece of newspaper on the floor. I dived beneath it and froze.

I looked up and saw that it was a photograph. I couldn't make sense of the photo, of course, it was just big black dots of ink. I could make out letters, each as big as my head.

<I'm clear,> Ax called. <I am with Cassie.>

Good. That was two of them safe. <Rachel? Marco?>

<I'm on a guy's sock,> Rachel reported. <He doesn't know I'm here. Wait. We're outside! I'm going to drop off! Clear! Clear! I'm outside!>

<Marco?>

<Yeah, Jake.>

<Where are you?>

<I am in a place where I really, really hope no one flushes, Jake.>

<You're in a toilet?>

<They have a bathroom. It seemed like a natural place for a roach. I'm chilling for a minute, then I'm going to try for the hole in the wall where the pipe goes. How about you?>

<I'm not so good. I'm under a newspaper, but they're still stamping all around. Sooner or later they'll stamp here. I have to make a run for it. I'm going to try for the door. Once I get outside they'll never get me in the dark.>

<Good luck, man,> Marco said.

<Yeah. You, too, my friend.>

Then, my antennae picked up a strange new scent. Sweet. Oily.

Dangerous. Somehow, I sensed that . . .

It hit me in a flash!

<Marco! They have bug spray!>

I blew out from under the paper.

"There! There's one!"

Vibrations of a dozen feet running after me. And in the air behind me, a vast fountain that seemed to explode from thin air.

An upside-down fountain. Like a rainfall that came from a single point and spread out to fill the air.

A droplet landed on me.

Then another.

I felt my legs stumble.

The door. I could sense it, just ahead.

WWHHAAMMPP!

A foot! A near miss. I was slowing down! I could feel my roach instincts becoming scrambled.

I was poisoned. The nerve gas was beginning to work. My legs were tangling up. My antennae were waving frantically, unable to smell anything but the deadly rain of poison.

"That got him!" a voice said.

"Don't crush him," Visser Three yelled. "He may demorph to save himself and we'll have ourselves an Andalite!"

I was starting to twitch. I couldn't breathe.

And then, faster by far than the feet that had chased me, some new shape swooped down.

I tried to run, but I no longer could.

Three monstrous cables closed around me, and I was up, up, off the floor.

<Hang in there, Jake,> Tobias said. <It's me. Red-tailed Airline welcomes you aboard, and I am hauling my feathers outta here!>

Chapter 10

<Morph, Jake! Morph now!>

Tobias had set me down on the roof of a Boston Market restaurant. It was the closest safe place he could find.

I was lying helpless on tar paper and gravel. My legs were twitching. My antennae waved insanely. I was twitching and jerking and losing all control over my roach body.

But the human me understood what was going on.

I was dying.

I had watched roaches die from poisoning. I had stood over them and thought, "Ha, serves you right."

Now it was me. Now it was my body that was

failing. I was the one suffocating and jerking.

<Jake! You have to morph out of this. Do it! Concentrate!>

I knew he was right. It was the only way to stay alive. But it was so hard to focus when I was trapped inside a dying body.

I tried to picture myself human. I tried to form a mental image of myself. But that picture was all mixed up with dolphins and birds and tigers.

And the dream . . .

I was in it now, as the delirium swept over me. In the dream . . .

I was the tiger. Moving with perfect silence. Each muscle like liquid steel. Every movement controlled, calculated.

I could smell my prey. I could hear his clumsy human movements in the dark forest. He was slow. He was weak. He could not escape me. I would destroy him. I would bring down my prey.

My prey . . . Tom.

I saw him turn to look at me. I saw fear in his eyes. Fear of me.

I settled back on my haunches, preparing for the final lunge. The killing lunge that would end with my teeth sinking into his neck. My jaws crushing his spine.

He looked at me and held up his hands. "No!"

I leapt, uncoiling unbelievable power. I leapt,

a huge, unstoppable hunter. I roared, a thunderous cry of triumph that could be heard for kilometres.

And then I saw the tiger. Saw myself. Saw orange striped fur and ruthless yellow eyes and sabre teeth and claws that could rip open a buffalo, hurtling towards *me.*

Tom had become the tiger. And I was his prey.

I closed my eyes. And when I opened them again, I saw, right above me, fierce eyes staring down from just a few centimetres away. The eyes of a hawk.

<Are you OK?> Tobias asked.

I raised my hand to look at it. Fingers. Five of them.

"I don't know? Am I OK?"

<You seem to have all your major limbs and so on,> Tobias said. <But it was a weird morph. You got poisoned pretty badly, I think. You seemed to be unconscious while you morphed.>

"I'm alive," I said, feeling a little surprised. But of course the amount of poison that had almost killed me when I was a roach was nothing to me as a human. "Where are we?"

<On the roof of a fast-food restaurant.>

"You saved my neck, Tobias."

<No problem. I am your own personal Air Force, dude. Just call in the air support any time you need it.>

I sat up. "How are the others?"

<Worried about you. I checked up on them while you were coming out of morph. They're scattered around, but OK. Everyone morphed back. Ax is already in human morph again. Cassie has him with her.>

"I guess I should get down from here," I said.

<Yeah,> Tobias agreed. <So. Marco told me what you found out. This is major.>

"Definitely major," I agreed. I stood up and began to look around for a way to escape from the roof. I was too tired and rattled to morph again.

<Marco says Visser Three was there. In a human morph. The guy who showed up in the limo, right?>

"Yeah, I guess so. I mean, roach eyes are pretty lame. I can only go by what I heard."

<I saw him leave, right after I lifted you out of there,> Tobias said.

I stopped looking for a ladder to the ground. Tobias was being too talkative. Too persistent.

"Tobias? What is it? What are you trying to get around to telling me?"

<When Visser Three left, Tom was with him.>

My first reaction was relief. Visser Three had ordered someone executed in that meeting. It had not been Tom.

"How, um . . . how did they look together? Visser Three and Tom?"

<Tom was the only one from the meeting who went with Visser Three, aside from his guards. Tom was acting sort of careful around Visser Three. But he looked like he was pretty cocky around the guards. It's hard to say, Jake. But if I had to guess, I'd say Tom and Visser Three are tight.>

"Yeah," I said. "I have a feeling maybe Tom is kind of responsible for a big part of this hospital plan." I shut up and thought for a second.

"What will Visser Three do to Tom if this great plan is destroyed?"

Tobias said nothing. He knew the answer.

Those who fail Visser Three die.

Chapter 11

I saw the lane open up between Juan and Terry. A clear lane to the basket.

Thonk. Thonk. Thonk. My right hand dribbled the ball. I stuck my left arm out, ready to ward off Juan if he came after me. I powered ahead.

Trainers squeaked on the polished wood floor of the gym. One of the guys on my team yelled, "Go, Jake!"

Juan saw my move and came after me. But I was just a little too fast. Thonk! Thonk! Thonk!

Stop. Pivot my back to Juan. Lock on to the basket, focus, focus . . .

I jumped and arced the ball towards the hoop.

It hit the backboard. It hit the rim. It bounced away. No score.

I fell back against Juan and Terry — the three of us ended up in a tangle on the gym floor, arms and legs everywhere. The ball rolled out of bounds.

"No wonder you never made the team," Terry said, laughing as he helped pull me to my feet.

I had tried out for the team, but I didn't make the cut. At the time it had bothered me. Mostly because Tom had been the big basketball hero when he was at our school. I wanted to live up to that.

Now, I realized I didn't have time for after-school sports anyway. And playing during gym class was enough basketball.

"Yeah? Well, I beat Juan with some of my excellent moves, and he *is* on the team," I said. I reached back to help pull Juan up. "Although I can't figure out why they would want some guy who looks like he's made out of straws."

"I'm just saving my best stuff for the finals," Juan said. "I don't want to waste my secret, killer moves on you, Jake. And now you practically crushed my legs, you big ox. Man, you ought to be playing football."

"Good idea." I grinned at Juan. He's about a hundred and eight centimetres and weighs like five kilogrammes. "Let me practise my tackling on you."

Just then the coach whistled, which was the signal to hit the showers.

"Saved by the whistle, Juan," I said.

"You should have inherited some of Tom's moves," Terry said. "That brother of yours has a jump shot."

"Man, Tom could have been in college ball easy. At a good school, too. If he would have stuck with it," Juan chimed in. "That boy has the gift."

They were right. Tom did have the gift. But he had dropped out of basketball. The Yeerk who controlled him had other plans, I guess.

I showered and got dressed for my next class. Marco was waiting out in the hallway. He had gym next period.

"B-ball today?" he asked. "Cool. I thought it was going to be more wrestling. I hate wrestling. Getting up close and personal with sweaty guys? Not my idea of a good time."

"The ancient Greeks used to wrestle with no clothes," I pointed out. "Just be glad this isn't Greece."

"And no deodorant," Marco agreed. "It's going to be next Tuesday."

"What's going to be next Tuesday?"

Marco looked over my shoulder and then, very casually, around the hallway to make sure no one was close enough to overhear. "The governor. That's when he's going in the hospital. I'll bet you a hundred bucks it's for haemorrhoids." He grinned. "That's why it's kind of secret. No one is supposed to know."

"So, how do *you* know?"

"Well, we know from the meeting the other night that he's going, right? So all I had to do is find out what his schedule is going to be. Turns out it's no problem. I told them I was a reporter and they faxed me a copy."

Marco pulled a folded piece of paper from his pocket and opened it for me to see.

"See? Saturday he gives a speech. Sunday he goes on a TV interview show. Monday he gives another speech. Tuesday . . . oops! Suddenly on Tuesday he begins a five-day holiday, and they don't say where he's going."

"Why would he keep it a secret, I wonder?"

"Oh, puh-leeze. If it is haemorrhoids? A politician getting his haemorrhoids operated on? The jokes are just too easy. Letterman would be talking about it in his monologue."

I smiled. "Yeah, OK. Good work."

"Tomorrow's Saturday," Marco said. "Should we do it then?"

I guess the expression on my face showed how I felt. Marco cocked his head and looked sideways at me. "You OK, man? You had a close call last night. I've been there, so I know it isn't easy to just get past it."

"No, I'm cool," I said. I gave him a push.

"Besides, since when are you all psyched to go?" Marco had always been the most reluctant member of the group.

"You know since when," he said softly.

I nodded.

Marco was no longer reluctant to fight the Yeerks. It had become a very personal battle for him.

"Yeah, sorry," I said.

"As far as the others are concerned, I'm still the same old Marco," he said. "I don't want them thinking anything is different. I don't want them feeling sorry for me."

"Now, Marco, how is anyone ever going to feel sorry for you? You're so totally obnoxious."

"And I plan to stay that way."

The bell rang, signalling the next class.

"OK," I said. "Tomorrow. We'll need to think of some way to get inside that hospital, though. They'll really be on the lookout."

"Actually, Cassie already suggested something to me," Marco said.

I rolled my eyes. "Oh, man. You know, I like Cassie. But this is the girl who suggested we try an ant morph."

Marco started to head into the gym. I headed towards class.

"Not ants," he said over his shoulder.

"I don't even want to know."

"Think dog dirt."

"What?" I demanded. But by then he was through the door and gone.

Chapter 12

"Something nice, but for fifteen bucks or less," I said. "My dad's birthday is in two months, so I have to spread my money pretty thin."

It was after school. We had headed to the shopping mall. Me and Cassie and Rachel. My mum's birthday was coming up. I had about fifteen dollars to buy her something, and the last time I'd bought her a present it hadn't turned out all that well.

Who would ever guess that she wouldn't appreciate a classic *Spiderman 3* in almost mint condition?

OK, so I was a year younger then. Plus, I had asked Marco to help me find something.

This time I asked Cassie if she would help

me shop. Which was almost as dumb, since Cassie isn't really into clothing and cute little stuff.

So Cassie had asked Rachel to help.

"How about *that* store?" I asked, pointing at one that had women's clothing.

"Yeah, right. Good choice, as long as you have at least a hundred dollars to spend," Rachel said.

"OK. How about . . ." Cassie began.

"Uh-uh. Cassie, think about it," Rachel said, looking slightly perturbed by our stupidity. "Look at the name of the store. It might as well scream 'fat, middle-aged ladies'. Jake? Do you want to tell your mum you think she's fat?"

"No." I shook my head vigorously. But then I thought it might be a trick question. "I mean, I don't, do I?"

Rachel rolled her eyes. "No, you don't. *Duh.* Have you two ever shopped for anything? I feel like I'm dealing with Ax here. I mean, are you two *from* this planet? We're looking for something on sale. Something that says 'Mum, I still think of you as being young and cool.' Something classic, understated. Most likely, we're talking a department store." She pointed. "That department store. Second floor. Towards the front, on the right. That's where we want to be. Look for sale signs. They'll be red with black letters."

Cassie grinned at me. "See? Rachel owns this mall."

"Shopping and kicking butt. Rachel's specialities," I said affectionately.

We cruised the department store and in about ten minutes, Rachel had found a silk blouse.

"It was thirty-three dollars originally," Rachel crowed. "Thirty-three, marked down to twenty-five. Then, a thirty per cent discount for this one-day sale. We got it for seventeen fifty! Do you realize that's almost half off the original price? Seventeen and a half bucks! For *that* blouse! Yes! She shops, she scores!"

"Yeah, but I was only going to spend fifteen," I said meekly.

"You didn't spend too much. Don't you know anything? You *saved* fifteen dollars and fifty cents. You came out ahead by more than fifteen bucks!"

"Wait a minute. How did I save, if I spent?"

Cassie put her hand on my arm. "No. Don't ask. Rachel uses a whole twisted maths involved in shopping. Don't even try and understand it."

Rachel ignored Cassie's teasing. "Hey. While you pay, I have to go and check something in Juniors. Meet you at the food court."

Rachel peeled off, leaving me and Cassie alone in the racks of clothing.

"So when are you going to tell me your

idea?" I asked.

"I thought Marco already told you."

I shook my head. "Nope. He just said 'think dog dirt.' I did. I got a very bad feeling as a result."

Cassie looked a little pouty. "Look, it was the only animal I could think of that could get in and out of a hospital without getting stepped on or poisoned. We wouldn't even be seen, probably. I mean, they go everywhere. Who even notices them?"

"Cassie, so far I have done three insects. Flea, that was OK. Ant, that was definitely not OK. And roach. I'm starting to feel jealous of Tobias. I mean, he's stuck as a hawk, but at least he doesn't have to go around turning into bugs."

"Do you have a better idea, Jake? Because I respect your feelings. I was just trying to help. It's just a suggestion."

I drew a deep breath. "No, I don't have any great suggestions. I'm just . . . I mean . . . it's just, whatever happened to the good old days when we would be tigers or wolves or something fun? I don't want to be a fly. I saw that movie. *The Fly.* Both versions. The old one, and the new one with Jeff Goldblum. I mean, a fly? A *fly*?"

"The movie. I forgot that movie," Cassie said. She made a face. "The one where the guy

has a tiny little human head stuck on a fly body and he's trapped in a spider's web and he's going *'h-e-e-e-l-p m-e-e-e'* in this little tiny voice? And that guy is so grossed out he just crushes him?"

We both just stood there, looking kind of sick.

"Moths?" Cassie suggested.

"Too slow," I said. "And too big. They would spot us."

"OK . . . um . . . bees?"

"No way. No social insects ever again. Bees could be as bad as ants that way. No social insects. No hives. No colonies." I shuddered at the memory of the ant morph. It had been like dying. The ant had no individual self. It was just a part of a bigger machine.

"Flies aren't social," Cassie said.

"Can I help you?" a saleswoman asked.

"No," Cassie said. "Thanks, anyway."

We started walking, heading to the food court to hook up with Rachel.

"It would just be to get into the hospital," I said, thinking out loud. "If they are using the hospital to transfer Yeerks into hosts, it will mean they have some kind of a Yeerk pool in there. That's what we are after. Find that Yeerk pool, wipe it out."

"So we would just be in fly morph for a brief time," Cassie said. "I mean, if we decided to do it. We'd have to demorph to do any damage."

"And then, if we create enough confusion, we can escape in some other way. We wouldn't have to do flies again."

"True," Cassie agreed. "We'd probably only be in the fly morph for a few minutes."

"Yep."

"So it's flies," Cassie said.

"Yep."

Then, both of us, at the same time, said *"H-e-e-e-l-p m-e-e-e! H-e-e-e-l-p m-e-e-e!"*

Chapter 13

Here's the thing about flies.

Being a fly is fun. It really is.

Turning into a fly . . . that is a *whole* different story.

I guess it's no big secret that I kind of like Cassie. I think she's really pretty. But when I saw these two huge, glittering, bulging, compound eyes come popping out of her eye sockets, I screamed.

I mean, I screamed like a baby.

"Yaaaaahhh!"

"Great, Jake. That's going to make her feel good," Marco said.

"Marco, *you* have your eyes closed," I pointed out.

“And they’re staying closed, too.”

“Excuse me,” Rachel said. She raced for the door of the barn and ran outside. A few seconds later we heard the sound of retching.

You have to understand. Cassie was mostly still human at the point where the fly eyes showed up. She was about a metre tall and shrinking fast, and the extra legs had already popped out of her chest, and the gauzy wings were growing from her back, but her face was still a *human* face.

Until the eyes popped out.

Oh, man. You think you’ve seen scary stuff? Maybe in movies or on TV? You haven’t seen anything scary till you’ve seen fly eyes pop out of someone’s head like a pair of balloons.

She was pretty small by the time her fly mouth appeared. I was grateful for that. Because later, when I became a fly, I saw what a fly mouth looks like.

The eyes were bad. But if I’d seen that long, tubular, sucking, tongue-like thing come rolling out . . . that thing that spits on the food, then sucks the spit mixture back in . . .

Rachel came back inside. “Sorry,” she said shakily. “Anyone have some gum? A Tic Tac?”

Ax was puzzled. <Does the morphing process disturb you?>

“Sometimes,” I said, still fighting the urge to

look away as Cassie shrivelled down to a few centimetres. "Some animals give me the willies."

<The willies? What are the willies?>

"Well, it's just this feeling of being grossed out. Sickened. Nauseated. Creeped. Like your skin is crawling. Willies."

<Is she done?> Tobias asked. <I'm not coming in there until she's done.>

"Tell Tobias it's OK, will you, Ax?"

<Tobias. Prince Jake says it's cool.>

I smiled at Marco, who was now peeking through his fingers. Ax was learning to sound semi-normal. At least in thought-speak. When he was in human morph and spoke out loud, he still played with every sound and drove everyone crazy.

Tobias flew in through the open hayloft above.

"Can you hear me, Cassie?" Rachel asked.

"Tobias. Do you see her?" Cassie was a true fly now.

<Got her.>

"Keep a sharp focus on her," I said. "Don't lose sight."

<Relax. It's broad daylight, she's three metres away. At this distance I can see the hairs on her little fly legs. Unfortunately. Ooooh. Oh, man. Oh, that's just not even slightly attractive.>

"Cassie?" Rachel asked again.

"Tobias? Try her with thought-speak."

<Cassie? Cassie, can you hear me? There she goes! She's flying!>

"Don't lose her, Tobias. Don't lose her."

"She won't go far," Marco said. "All the horse manure in this barn? Where would she go that's any better for a fly?"

Suddenly, in my head I heard <Yeeeeee haaaaahhhh!>

"Cassie?"

<Cassie?>

<Whooooo hoooooo!>

"Cassie! Answer us!"

<Cassie? You OK?>

<Oh, man! Man! Can this thing fly! You guys have got to try this. This thing flies like a rocket. Yaaaah haaaahhh!>

<Are you able to control the fly brain?>

<Yes, yes. Don't worry, you guys. I'm fine. Sorry. But it's just such a complete, insane rush! Come on, let's go, time's a-wasting.>

I sucked in a deep breath. I had been hoping everything would be fine. That Cassie would not have any problems. But at the same time, I was utterly disgusted at the idea of becoming a fly. And now she was saying it was OK.

You'd think it would get easier, slipping in and out of strange shapes. But you'd be wrong. Gross is gross, and always remains gross.

"OK, guys. It looks like we're doing this," I said, trying desperately to sound cheerful and optimistic.

"Oh, goody," Marco said.

<Yes! Goody!> Ax said, totally unaware that Marco was being sarcastic.

"Sounds like Cassie's having fun," Rachel said.

"Uh-huh," I said. "Let's just do it."

We did it.

Morphing was as gross as we'd expected.

But Cassie was also right. Once you were in the morph; once you got used to the fact that your vision was like a thousand tiny TV screens, each showing a slightly different picture; once you got done freaking about the way your nasty fly tongue stuck out; once you got past the bizarre combination of hooks and bristles and hairs that made up your fly leg; once you got past the fact that nothing looks right or familiar when you're only about three millimetres long; and mostly, once you stopped thinking about that stupid fly movie . . .

Well, then, it was cool!

I have flown before. As a peregrine falcon and as a seagull.

Both are cool. I mean, the falcon can go like two hundred and eighty kilometres an hour in a dive.

Faster than a stock car. Faster than small planes.

But flying as a fly is totally, completely insane.

A housefly beats its wings 200 times per second.

Say "hello, there" out loud. In the time it took you to say that, a fly's wings beat 200 times.

A fly moves at about six kilometres per hour. Which doesn't sound very fast, compared to a falcon hitting almost three hundred and twenty kilometres per hour. But trust me, when you're only three millimetres long, six kilometres an hour is like warp factor nine.

And what's really cool is you can do that going down, going left, right, or straight up.

And you can change directions in no time. One minute you're shooting straight ahead like a bullet, the next tenth of a second you're going straight up.

Cassie was right. It was gross, but it was fun.

<Yeeeee haaaaahhh!> Ax yelled.

<Whoooaaaa hooaaahhh!> I cried as I blasted straight up at what felt like the speed of light.

<We are ugly as sin, but we are so cool!> Rachel exulted.

<Let's go find some dog dirt!> Marco said. <Kidding,> he added a second later. <Just kidding.>

<OK, OK, we have important stuff to do,> I said after we had all spent a couple of minutes getting used to the fly's simple instincts and pretty decent senses. <Time to get on the bus.>

Tobias was the bus. The hospital was a couple of kilometres away. Flies are fast in *relative* terms, but in actual speed, Tobias was a lot quicker. It would have taken us hours. Tobias could carry us there in a few minutes.

<Hop on the big feathery guy,> Cassie said. <Aim for the back of his neck. We don't want his wings or tail knocking us off.>

<It's just a good thing I know you guys,> Tobias said. <My own little necklace of house-flies. It's enough to gag a maggot.>

<Gag a maggot?> Marco echoed. <Gag a *maggot*? Hey pal, don't be slagging our kids that way.>

<Yuck,> Tobias commented. And then we were off.

Chapter 14

I clung to Tobias's feathers. It was easy enough to do. Fly legs can grab on to glass, or hang upside down on a ceiling.

I could feel the wind whipping around me. It rattled my wings and actually whistled through the chinks and joints of my tiny exoskeleton.

An incredible array of aromas assaulted my sensitive antennae. Unfortunately, the main things my fly brain seemed interested in were anything sweet, anything rotting, or anything decayed and putrid.

<This is a little like that shrew morph I did early on,> Rachel pointed out. <The same interest in dead meat.>

Suddenly, a monster! It loomed huge in my

compound eyes. Smaller than me, but still way, way too big.

<What the . . . !> I yelped.

<What? What is it?> Cassie asked.

<Oh, man. I think it's a flea. It looks about the size of a poodle. But not even slightly cute.>

<Wait a minute!> Tobias cried. <Are you telling me I have fleas?>

<Just one that I've seen,> I answered. <Now he's gone. He probably jumped off.>

Actually, I was lying. The flea was working his way along Tobias skin, beneath the feathers, looking for a good place to sink his penetrating, bloodthirsty tongue.

But somehow I didn't think Tobias would want to hear that.

<OK, we're at the hospital,> Tobias said. <I'll take a low pass, then tell you guys when to jump off. Kind of like an old war movie. You guys are the paratroopers.>

<Good example,> Marco said. <Ever notice how in those old movies the paratroopers mostly get shot?>

<Jake?> Cassie whispered to me in thought-speak so that no one else could hear.

<Yeah?>

<You could still drop out of this mission,> she said. <Everyone would understand.>

<Thanks. But no. Tom or no Tom, the Yeerks

have to be stopped.> That's what I told myself, anyway. I guess it was true.

<OK, everything looks fine to me,> Tobias said. <I see an open window on the third floor. No screen.>

<You're sure?> Marco asked.

<Marco, in light this bright I could tell you if there was a single strand of spider's web across that window, let alone a screen.>

<He said spider's web,> Rachel moaned.

<*H-e-e-e-l-p m-e-e-e!*> Marco mimicked.

By absolutely terrible luck, the old version of *The Fly* had been on TV the night before. Like fools, we'd all watched it.

<I don't understand what this means,> Ax grumbled.

<Get ready,> Tobias said. <Three . . . two . . . one . . . bail!>

I leapt from his back. I opened my wings. The slipstream was so fast it sent me tumbling, end over end through the air. But as my speed dropped I quickly gained control.

<Everyone OK?>

<Yee hah!> Rachel said.

<I see the window opening,> Ax said.

I saw him fly past me like a buzzing, wobbling, careening jet fighter. At least I think it was him. I fell in behind, following his wake.

It turned out Ax was wrong. What he'd

thought was a window was actually a small sign on the side of the building. With fly eyes you had to get pretty close to see anything. So we blazed along the face of the building for a while, trying to spot it.

<Keep going,> Tobias called to us. <You're almost there.>

Suddenly, I could feel a rush of cooler air, billowing out at us.

<Here we go,> I said.

I turned into the current of air and seconds later was in the relative darkness inside the building.

<OK. We're looking for anything that might be a miniature Yeerk pool,> I reminded everyone. <Everyone except Ax has been near a Yeerk pool, so try to remember that smell, and see if your antennae pick up anything similar.>

<I'll tell you one thing. I'll bet I know where the maternity ward is. I smell large numbers of dirty nappies,> Rachel said.

<OK, let's split up, like we planned. Ax and Cassie, you're with me. Rachel and Marco, be careful.>

Rachel and Marco peeled off and soon disappeared from sight.

The three of us flew out into what we figured was a hallway, since it seemed very long and had bright lights all along it.

<I smell poop. I smell a banana. At least, I think it's a banana. And, I smell more poop,> Cassie said. <Say one thing for flies. If you ever need to find poop, hire a fly.>

Below us, barely visible, we occasionally caught sight of big, moving oval shapes — the tops of people's heads. But with our limited sight, they seemed like floating islands of hair moving on a blurry sea.

<How's our time, Ax?> I asked.

<We have used twenty per cent of our time,> Ax reported.

<Good. That's right on plan,> I said, trying to reassure myself as much as the two of them.

<Yaaaahhh!>

<What is it?>

<That human tried to reach up and hit me!> Ax said. <But he was very slow.>

<Hey,> Cassie said. <Hey. Do you guys smell that?>

<More poop?>

<No. Similar to poop, but different. A strange smell. My fly brain doesn't know what it is. I'm trying to remember . . .>

<I too am smelling something,> Ax reported. <But not very strong.>

<I'm thinking we turn right,> Cassie suggested.

<Right turn,> I agreed. Now I was getting

the scent, too. A dark, deep, rich aroma. Sweet and oily.

<Marco, Rachel,> I called to them in thought-speak. <You guys have anything?>

<Barely hear —— must —— away. Nothing ——>

<We are at the limits of the thought-speak range,> Ax said.

Now the scent was more powerful than before.

<In there,> I said. <I think that's a door.>

We landed. My six legs, each armed with sharp talons and sticky pads, gripped the smooth surface of the door.

<Here's a question,> Cassie said. <How do you open a door when you're like three millimetres?>

<Down to the floor. We can walk or fly under the crack.>

Seconds later, we were on the linoleum, marching jerkily forward. We passed beneath the door, then instantly took flight again.

<Oh, man, there is definitely something in here,> Cassie said. <Over there. Do you see a big, shiny-looking superdome kind of thing?>

<Yeah. I agree. I think that may be it. Does anyone see anyone in the room? Any humans?>

No one did.

<OK, Ax. You demorph first. If someone

barges in, your Andalite body will be more useful than the two of us as humans.>

<Yes, Prince Jake.>

<Ax? You really, really don't have to call me that.>

<Yes, Prince Jake. I am beginning the change.>

<Cool. Cassie and I will hang out on the ceiling.>

A few moments later I saw a vast eyeball, stuck on the end of a long stalk, come shooting up towards us where we hung upside down. One of Ax's extra, stalk-mounted eyes. The eye turned to look at us.

Then, a violent vibration in the air. The eye disappeared from sight.

And a second vibration, like something heavy falling.

<Ax? Are you OK?>

<Yes. There was a human here. But he is unconscious now.>

Chapter 15

We demorphed as quickly as we could. When my human eyesight returned, I saw Ax, standing calmly in his Andalite form. Against the far wall was a man in a white coat, holding a clipboard.

He was crumpled and unconscious, but alive.

<Knowing your brother is a Controller, I did not kill this creature,> Ax said. <I feared it might be him.>

"No. It's not. But that's a good instinct, Ax. Whoever this guy is, he's someone's brother or son or even father."

I took a look first at my own body. I was barefoot, like I always was when I came out of a morph. And wearing only my silly-looking bike shorts and tight T-shirt. (Even Ax can't figure out how to morph anything more than the most minimal clothing.) But I seemed to have all my usual legs and arms.

"You OK, Cassie?" I asked.

"I'm fine." She pointed at what had looked like a shiny superdome to us as flies. It was a stainless steel vat about two and a half metres across.

I laughed. "You know what this is? This is a whirlpool. A Jacuzzi. Someone just put a lid over it. Why would they have this in a hospital?"

"For therapy," Cassie said. "You know, for people with muscle strains or back problems."

I stepped to the side of the whirlpool. I grabbed the handles on the lid and lifted. It opened easily on hydraulic hinges. I looked inside. I recoiled.

The water was sludgy, brown, and viscous.

And roiling with slugs.

Yeerks. In their natural state.

"Well, well, well," I said.

<Yeerks,> Ax said, with that combination of disgust and pure hatred Andalites always showed. <A portable Yeerk pool. There must be a small Kandrona nearby.>

Yeerks must leave their host bodies every three days to return to a Yeerk pool. In the Yeerk pool they feed by soaking up various nutrients, but especially Kandrona rays, which are like the

rays of their home sun. Kandronas are artificial sources of Kandrona rays.

"Can they see us? Now, I mean?"

<No, Prince Jake. In their natural state they are blind.>

I walked slowly around the whirlpool. My foot hit something solid. The pump for the whirlpool action. It was disconnected, with a wire pulled out of the wall socket. The control panel had been ripped away, exposing bare wires.

"Ax? What do you think would happen to all those Yeerks in there if the temperature of the liquid suddenly went up to say, one hundred and twenty degrees? And the liquid was all agitated?"

Ax looked puzzled. <I believe the heat and the agitation might destroy them.>

"Well. That would be a pity." I made a quick decision. "Ax? Watch the door to the hallway. Cassie? We may need you in some more dangerous morph. What have you got?"

"Wolf?"

"Perfect. But no howling."

"What are you going to do?" Cassie asked.

"We came here to stop this sick operation, right? Well, wiping out a hundred or so Yeerks might be a good way to start. I'm going to hook this thing back together, and Jacuzzi these filthy creeps to death."

There were no tools in the room. But I did

find some tape and a pair of tweezers. That was all I needed. I began reconnecting wires, red to red, blue to blue, green to green. Without the switches, the settings would all automatically be at maximum. Maximum heat, maximum jets.

But all the while, in the back of my head, was this nagging feeling.

It couldn't be this easy.

I connected the last wire.

Cassie had finished the transformation into her wolf body. She stood by patiently, like a very big, very tough-looking dog.

"OK. Time to boil some Yeerks."

I reached down and stuck the plug in the outlet.

It took a few seconds, then the boiling sound began. The familiar Jacuzzi bubbling.

The door opened. A man and a woman, both wearing white lab coats. For a split second they just froze and stared.

"Andalite!" the woman yelped.

Cassie was on her in a flash. She leapt, hit the woman hard, and knocked her to the floor.

Ax moved towards the man, but the man was fast. He dodged, staying out of range of Ax's tail.

I was still behind the whirlpool, out of sight. I was trying to focus on morphing into tiger form for a fight.

But then, two more men, dressed in uniform

as guards, came ploughing into the room. The first one levelled a gun.

"Ax!" I shouted. "A gun!"

Ax's tail flashed.

"Aaaargghh!" the Controller screamed.

The hand that had been holding the gun was no longer attached to the man's arm.

"Get backup to the pool area! Andalites!" the second guard screamed into a walkie-talkie. Then he drew his gun.

BLAM! BLAM!

They told me later there was a third shot. But I didn't hear it.

A sledgehammer blow struck the side of my head. A ricochet. For a brief second I clung to consciousness. But then, I swooned. I fell.

Face down in the whirlpool.

Face down in the bubbling, boiling mass of dying Yeerks.

Chapter 16

Face down, unconscious, in the superheating Yeerk pool.

I don't know for how long.

When I woke I had two terrifying, overwhelming feelings. One was suffocation. I had breathed in a lungful of the liquid from the pool.

I came to, gasping and hacking and gagging. I was alive, but I could hardly breathe. Each breath was a struggle. I coughed and I think at one point I threw up.

The second feeling was of pain in my head. Pain like nothing I had ever even imagined before. It was like someone was drilling a hole in my ear, drilling straight into my brain.

I wanted to scream, but I was still choking. I

was on my knees on the floor of the hospital room, wanting to cry from the pain and gasping for every half-breath of air.

All the while, a battle raged. They were trying to get in the doorway. But it was too narrow for more than one or two human-Controllers at a time to attack. Ax's tail and Cassie's long wolf teeth were enough to hold them off.

BLAM! Another gunshot!

"Stop firing, you fool!" someone shouted. "The pool is in there! Visser Three will eat your guts!"

Even in my condition I could see that Ax and Cassie couldn't last. I needed to morph, to join the battle. But I could not seem to do it. The pain . . . or maybe the lack of oxygen . . . I couldn't concentrate. My brain was fuzzy, drifting . . .

I heard a rumbling, pounding noise from the hallway outside. There were cries and screams of rage. Suddenly, into the room burst a huge black gorilla and a second wolf.

Marco and Rachel.

They had driven the attackers away, but only for a few seconds.

<Jake's hurt,> I heard Cassie say. <He fell in the Yeerk pool.>

<Marco, grab Jake,> Rachel ordered. <Get something to cover his face. Ax, Cassie, keep

holding the door. I'm going to change morph. We need more firepower.>

I felt myself lifted up off the floor. A white cloth was wrapped around my head. One of the lab coats from an injured Controller, I guessed. I was cradled in the huge arms of a gorilla.

<Rock-a-bye baby,> Marco joked. <Hang in there, man. We're getting you out of here.>

I was still coughing and gasping, but my breathing was at least improving. Not enough to speak, but I could breathe enough to keep from passing out.

At the same time, something had happened to the pain in my head. It was diminishing. And yet, instead of feeling more clear-headed, I felt more confused.

"Get them!" a Controller was yelling outside the door. "Attack. Attack!"

<It doesn't look like I'm gonna fit through this doorway.> It was Rachel. <So I guess I'll have to make the door a little bigger.>

I caught just a glimpse through the fabric that hid my face. A flash of something huge and grey.

Rachel's elephant morph.

<Rachel?> a voice in my head wondered. The voice was surprised. <A human?>

BOOOM! WHUMP! CRRRUUUUNNCH!

<Now the door is plenty big,> Rachel said.

Wild screams! Panic! Cries of pain!

I was bounced and slammed against walls and even dropped at one point. I felt us go down a set of stairs. I felt hands grabbing at me and slipping away.

Finally, fresh air. We were running like mad for the shelter of a stand of trees that fronted the hospital.

<Cassie!> Marco said. <You have a horse morph, right? Quick. Before they figure out how to follow us.>

I was tossed on to the dirt.

The gorilla peeled back the coat that was over my face. <You alive? Man! That was intense. That is one hospital that's going to need some redecorating. We're gonna put you on Cassie. Then we'll try to cover your retreat.>

"My . . . head . . ." I said.

<Headache? No surprise, dude.>

"Something . . . wrong . . . I can't . . . think."

<Don't worry. Take a break. We have it under control. More or less.>

<Unbelievable,> said a voice in my head. <Can it be? *Humans*?>

What was that voice? Where was it coming from?

Marco lifted me and slung me over a horse's back. Cassie.

<Cassie? A human, yes. And Rachel? The

cousin? Human as well.>

My hand tried to pull the coat away from my face.

What was happening? There was a voice inside my head.

We were running now, running and running at full gallop, through trees, across lawns, down suburban streets where Cassie's hooves clattered loudly.

We jumped a fence. I flew through the air and landed hard on the dirt.

I felt pain, but it came from far away.

The coat was loose. I looked around. Trees, everywhere. A panting horse standing nearby.

I saw all this, but in a distant way, as if I were watching it all on TV. My eyes moved left, right. They moved all on their own. Like someone else was focusing them.

Cassie. I tried to say her name. Cassie.

But no sound came from my mouth.

<Don't struggle, Jake,> a voice in my head said. <It's pointless.>

What? Who was saying that? What was . . . ?

Then, a laugh only I could hear. <Put that primitive human brain to work, Jake. Jake, the Animorph,> it sneered. <Jake, the servant of the Andalite filth!>

Then I knew.

I knew what the voice was.

A Yeerk!
A Yeerk in my own head.
I was a Controller.

Chapter 17

<Very good. You figured it out,> said the silent voice in my head, mocking me.

<NO! NO! NO!>

<Jake, are you all right?> Cassie asked. For a moment I thought she had heard me cry out. But no, she was just concerned.

Tobias landed on a branch overhead. <Is he OK?>

<I can't tell. He's alive. He's breathing. But it's like he's zoned out or something. We may have to take him to a doctor.>

I wanted to tell them both. To scream "They have me! They are inside me!" But I couldn't make my mouth move. It was like there was a roadblock. Like I could form the thoughts, give

the order to my lips and tongue to speak, but the order never got there.

<Struggle all you like, human. Fight me!> the Yeerk gloated. <Go ahead. It won't matter, in the end. I am in your head. I am wrapped around your brain like a living blanket.>

<NO!>

<I can read your thoughts. I control your body. I am tapped into your memory. I can read it like a book.>

<Get out of my head! No! No!>

<Oh, I don't think I want to do that, Jake. Why would I abandon such an interesting host? So you are the one who has driven Visser Three half-mad with rage. A kid. The midget.>

<*Midget*? How do —>

<You're surprised I know what Tom calls you? Ha ha ha. Oh, the irony really is sweet. Don't you get it, clever Jake? Don't you see what's happened, my little *Animorph*?>

Cassie had become human again. She knelt down beside me and looked down into my eyes. "He's alert. His eyes are tracking. Jake? Jake, can you talk to me?"

It was a nightmare. That's what it was. Another nightmare. I would wake up soon. I would wake up and laugh and laugh.

<I am Temrash one-one-four,> the Yeerk said proudly. <Formerly Temrash two-five-two, of the

Sulp Niar pool. I have been promoted. No doubt you are happy for me.>

<You filthy slug! Get out of my head!>

<Do you know what my last host was? *Who* it was?> the Yeerk taunted.

<Shut up! Shut up! Stop talking to me! Go away.> It wasn't real. It couldn't be real!

<It was Tom, of course. Your brother. I am the Yeerk who controlled your brother.>

That cut through my growing hysteria. <What?>

<Ah, I thought that might interest you. Yes, Tom was my host.>

<Then . . . he's . . .>

<Free? Ha ha ha.> The Yeerk laughed in my head. <You're even stupider than your brother. No, your brother's body has been given to a new Yeerk. Someone with a lower rank. I am too important now to be wasted on Tom. I am to take on a new and important project. A very special host.>

<The governor!>

<Jake,> Tobias tried thought-speaking to me. <If you can hear me, move your hand.>

<Well, well. Not a complete idiot, are you?> the Yeerk said. <Yes. I was to be given the most important post on this planet. But this is better still. Visser Three is very determined to catch you and your friends. He will be surprised to

learn that you are human.>

<I'll never tell you who the —>

<The others? You mean, Cassie, Marco, Rachel? Tobias, who's sitting in the tree over our heads? And of course the one remaining Andalite, Aximili Esgarrouth Isthill?>

"We have to get him to a doctor," Cassie told Tobias.

Just then, Marco arrived. He was fully human again. He was dressed in his morph clothes and walking gingerly without shoes. "Doctor? He needs a doctor? What's the matter with him?"

"Nothing is the matter with me," I said, quite suddenly. "I'm fine."

Only I didn't say it. My mouth spoke the words. But I didn't say it.

The Yeerk had spoken through my mouth.

"No way," Cassie said. "We're taking you to a doctor. You didn't answer me for like five minutes. Maybe you have concussion."

My body sat up. "Sorry I scared you, Cassie. But I'm fine. And where are you going to take me? Back to that hospital? What if some doctor does a blood test and he sees something that shows him I'm an Animorph?"

"Like what?" Marco asked, sounding sceptical.

"How do I know? Maybe some left-over roach DNA. Look, I'm fine, OK?"

<I'm going back up,> Tobias said. <Make

sure no one is after us, and see if Rachel and Ax are OK.> He flapped his wings and flew away through the trees.

"As soon as we know Rachel and Ax are safe, we need to break up and go our separate ways," my mouth said.

The Yeerk was considering his next move. I could not "hear" his thoughts. But I could feel him using my brain. He was digging through my memory. Trying to learn quickly about the others.

He was using my brain. Using me.

I had to do something quick. Something to warn Cassie and Marco. Surely they would guess what was happening. They were the two people in the whole world who were closest to me.

Surely they would realize that I was no longer myself.

Wouldn't they?

"I don't think there's all that much the Yeerks can do right now," Marco said to Cassie. "We're deep in the national forest. It would take a while for them to organize a search. They'd need helicopters and lots of human-Controllers. And they don't even know what they're looking for." He laughed. "After all, they still think we're Andalites."

"Yeah, but it means we're going to have to be very careful with Ax," my mouth said. "We'll need to hide him. I think we may have parboiled

quite a few Yeerks in that whirlpool. They're going to be *very* upset."

It was incredible. It was shocking to listen to. The Yeerk was using my voice. My inflection. He was saying the words I would have said.

Marco and Cassie would never guess. As far as they could see or hear, the Yeerk in my brain *was* me.

<Yes, little human,> the Yeerk sneered silently. <Your body is my home now. Mine. Body and mind, under my control. Forget resistance. It is futile. No host has ever overpowered a Yeerk. It is impossible.>

I felt a dark wave of terror wash over me. He was telling the truth. I knew he was. No host had ever defeated a Yeerk.

Resistance was futile.

Futile.

I would never be free. Just like Tom. If this Yeerk moved on, they would give me to another. I was a slave.

For ever.

There was a noise behind me. Footsteps on the pine needles and leaves. At the same time, Tobias came swooping down to land on a nearby branch.

I turned around. Rachel.

"Hey, cousin," I said. "I see you made it OK."

Then, a touch on my shoulder.

I spun suddenly. I hadn't heard anyone else arriving.

Ax! Just behind me. His Andalite face close to mine. His big eyes watching me.

And in that split second, hatred revealed itself. A hatred that had crossed light years of space to play itself out on planet Earth.

<Andalite!> the Yeerk hissed silently. And in that one word I heard the same fury and contempt I heard whenever Ax said the word "Yeerk."

Only I heard it. The Yeerk did not *say* a thing.

But surprised, unaware, unprepared, he did curl my lip in an instinctive expression of revulsion.

It was a small thing. It lasted only a second. And then the Yeerk was using my mouth to say, "Hey, Ax. You did great back there when —"

In a movement too fast for me to see, Ax whipped his tail forward. In the blink of an eye, his scythe blade was levelled just millimetres from my throat.

<Yeerk!> he said.

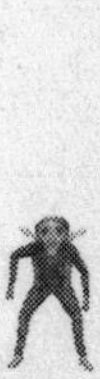

Chapter 18

"Ax! What are you doing?" Cassie demanded.

"Are you NUTS?" Marco cried.

"What's your problem, Ax?" my voice asked the Andalite.

But he did not waver. And he did not pull that deadly tail away from my throat. <Prince Jake has been taken. He is a Controller.>

"What?" Rachel snapped. "Back off, Ax. You're crazy."

<His head was in the Yeerk pool long enough for a Yeerk to enter his head,> Ax said. <And just now . . . you all saw his expression when he was surprised to see me. I am not human. I do not know every human expression. So tell me. What was that look?>

"This is crazy." The Yeerk tried a disbelieving laugh. "Marco . . . Cassie . . . would you please tell this nut that I am OK?"

But I saw doubt in Marco's shrewd eyes. "Yeah, I'm sure you're fine, Jake. But Cassie? Didn't you say Jake seemed zoned out? Like he wouldn't answer for a few minutes, even though he was awake?"

Cassie nodded her head. She, too, was looking suspicious. "Yeah. He seemed normal and all, but he wouldn't answer me." She shrugged. "Sorry, Jake, but you did act funny."

<It takes a while for the Yeerk to take full control of the host brain,> Ax said. <During that time the host will be passive. He may even seem to be in a coma.>

I swear, I could have kissed the Andalite right then. I wanted to yell "Yes! Yes!"

"You guys can't possibly believe this," my mouth said. "I mean, OK, we have to be careful. But it's me. It's me, Jake, all right?"

"Being Jake and all, you'll understand if we take a minute to think this through," Rachel said. "Ax? How are we supposed to know one way or the other?"

Tobias answered for him. <The Yeerk needs to return to the Yeerk pool and absorb Kandrona rays every three days. If we hold him for three days, we'll know.>

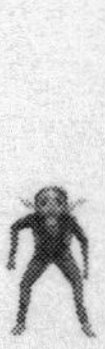

Now I felt just the slightest edge of fear from the Yeerk. He was measuring the odds. Trying to decide what to do. But with Ax's tail blade at my throat, the Yeerk kept my body very still.

"We can't hold him for three days," Cassie argued. "His family would go ballistic. They'll call the cops. Chapman will realize he's not in school. The bad guys will put two and two together."

"Look. Hello. Hello-o-o? It's me, Jake. Remember? I am not a Controller."

Marco shook his head. "If he is . . . if there's a Yeerk in his head, then he knows all our secrets. If he gets in touch with any other Yeerk, we are all dead. We can't take the chance. Maybe Ax is right. Maybe not. But we can't guess wrong."

<I agree,> Tobias said. <If he's still Jake, he'll understand. If he's a Controller, well, I guess we'll find out, won't we?>

"Rachel?" Marco asked.

Rachel met my gaze. "Sorry, Jake. But we have to play it safe. You know that."

"Look," I argued. "It's like Cassie said. My folks will go nuts. They'll call the police. They'll go on TV asking if anyone has seen me. They'll be putting up posters all over town. I mean, no offence, Tobias, but I have an actual family, not some messed-up aunts and uncles who didn't want to be taking care of me in the first place. People will notice if I disappear." I turned to Cassie. "Cassie, come on. Explain it to them."

Come on, Cassie, I thought. *Come on, be hard for once. Don't feel for me. Don't be sweet, just this once.*

"There is a way," Cassie said hesitantly.

"To be sure whether he's a Controller?" Rachel asked.

"No," Cassie said. Her voice grew stronger. "A way to keep his family and the school from knowing he's gone. Ax could do it. Ax could morph into Jake."

Cassie. The amazing Cassie. She had hit on the one possible solution. I wished so badly I could tell her right then what an amazingly smart, incredibly cool person she was.

The Yeerk in my head was not happy.

<What's the matter, Temrash one-one-four of the Sulp Niar pool?> I asked. <Not feeling quite so cocky any more?>

Ax reached one of his delicate, many-fingered hands towards my face. He pressed his fingers against my forehead.

<I will acquire your DNA now Prince Jake,> he said.

The Yeerk could not stand it any more. The Andalite's touch made him so furious it was like a physical illness.

"Get your hand off me, Andalite filth!" he screamed aloud in a distorted version of my voice.

But Ax's tail was still within a centimetre of my jugular. And the Yeerk knew very well how deadly fast that tail was. He did not move.

The others all stared, wide-eyed.

"Well," Rachel said. "At least now we're sure."

"No, you're wrong," my voice pleaded. "He's just making me mad. Hey, it's been a stressful morning, all right? Give me a break."

<'Andalite filth'?> Tobias repeated the Yeerk's words. <We're supposed to believe Jake would say that? Jake? Because he was stressed out? Nah. Not in this universe.>

"Jake," Cassie said, looking into my eyes. "I know you're still in there. I know you're probably afraid. But we will get that thing out of your head, Jake. We will."

Chapter 19

"OK," Marco said. "We need a place to keep him."

"We can't use anyone's home," Cassie said, thinking aloud. "We can't use my barn. My dad is in and out of there constantly."

<I know a place,> Tobias said. <It's not far from here. An old shack back in the woods.>

"We can tie him up," Rachel said. "But we'll still have to have at least one of us there all the time, to make sure he doesn't get away."

<I cannot help very much,> Ax said. <I will be pretending to be Jake.>

"OK," Marco said, "then the rest of us, Cassie, Rachel and I, will rotate shifts, along with Tobias. Tobias can stay the whole time, except when he has to go hunting."

"OK, let's go," Rachel said. "Come on, Jake. Get up. We're out of here."

Cassie came over and gave me her hand. She helped pull me to my feet.

It was an odd moment, because I could feel Cassie's touch. And yet I had no power to squeeze her hand, or give her any assurance.

The Yeerk did that for me. He deliberately held her hand an extra few seconds.

<She cares for you,> the Yeerk said. <She is their weak link. Rachel will be strong. So will the hawk and the Andalite. But Marco . . . he thinks too much. And he has an interesting history. He is open to persuasion.>

I felt sick. The Yeerk was opening my mind at will. Reading whatever he wanted. I had no secrets from him. None. He already knew everything I knew about my friends. If he got away . . .

My feet began walking. Tobias led the way, appearing and disappearing in the trees above.

Rachel walked ahead of me. Behind me, Marco and Ax. Cassie stayed at my side.

"From all we know, Jake, you can still hear me and understand me," Cassie said. "I know you can't answer. Or if you do answer it won't be you, anyway —"

"But it is me," said the Yeerk. "Who *else* would it be?"

"The Yeerk," Cassie said calmly.

"You think I'm a Controller just because I yelled at Ax? Like I've never lost my temper before? Come on. It was a bad day. For all of us, but especially for me."

<Not so bad a day,> Ax piped up from behind. <How many Yeerks were in that pool? How many survived those temperatures? Only you, by getting inside Prince Jake. How many of your pool-fellows died today?>

I could feel the Yeerk boiling with rage. It was shocking and bizarre to feel so much emotion. It was something he could not hide from me. I could *feel* his emotions, even though I could not penetrate his thoughts.

"Ax," the Yeerk said, "I'm never happy when any creature has to be destroyed. But I don't feel any pity for those Yeerks. They are out to enslave us. We did what we had to do."

It was perfect. Exactly what I would have said. Because it was exactly what I felt.

Out of the corner of my eye, I saw Cassie looking at me with a puzzled expression.

<See? Already she has doubts,> the Yeerk said to me. <She is bothered by the Andalite's bloodthirstiness. She liked what I said more.>

Was he right? Would all of my friends stand firm? How could they, when every word I spoke sounded exactly like me?

We marched through the woods for what seemed like a very long time. None of us could move very fast because we were without shoes. Tobias knew these woods well and led us around brambles and rough patches, but still, my feet were tender after an hour of walking on pine needles and twigs.

But the pain was so far away. . . . I was feeling it from a distance. It was like I was shackled. Chained to a wall. I could not move a hand, or even a finger. I did not blink my own eyes. I did not decide which direction to look, or what sounds to focus on.

The Yeerk's control was absolute.

<Almost there,> Tobias said. <I'm going higher to make sure the area is completely clear.>

<All this walking. Such a waste of effort,> the Yeerk commented to me. <They cannot possibly hold me against my will. Not even for three hours, let alone three days.>

"You heard Tobias, right, Jake?" Cassie asked. "Almost there. It's a good thing. My feet are killing me. I need to walk barefoot more often. Like I did when I was little. Toughen up, for times like these. Getting home will be easier. I can just use my osprey morph and fly home."

"Cassie, listen," the Yeerk said. "I know you guys think you're doing the right thing. But there's no way Ax can pull off being me. My parents will figure it out. Or worse yet, Tom will figure it out. Then we'll all be dead. Don't you see what's happening here?"

"Shut up, Yeerk," Rachel snapped. "I've known Jake all my life. Marco has known him since they were kids. And Cassie has known him for years. Between the three of us, we can teach Ax to pass for Jake."

"It will never work," the Yeerk said.

Rachel stopped walking. She turned to face me, blocking the way. She was smirking, but she seemed to be looking past me, over my shoulder. "No? You don't think so, Yeerk?"

The Yeerk stopped walking. "Rachel, you don't have to try and impress me with how tough you are. I know you're too smart to really believe any of this. And you know as well as I do, this is not going to work."

"I disagree," a voice behind me said. "Humans believe what they see."

The Yeerk whipped my head around.

There, standing two metres from me was . . . me.

Totally, absolutely, *me*.

Chapter 20

He was a perfect copy of me. Like looking in a mirror.

"I morphed a while back," Ax said. "I've been watching the way you walk and move. To copy you better. Ter. Bet. Ter."

The Yeerk grinned. "You may look like me, but that isn't going to be enough. I give it an hour before Tom figures it out."

Marco looked at Rachel and cocked an eyebrow. Rachel looked at Cassie, who sighed and nodded her head.

"See, that was a stupid way to play it, Yeerk," Marco said. "If you really were Jake, you might be frustrated that we wrongly suspected you. But you'd figure the smart thing would be to help Ax play the role. If you were you, so to speak, you'd have to hope Ax pulled it off."

Rachel curled her lip contemptuously. "You just blew final *Jeopardy.* You're still trying to make us let you go. By now Jake would have realized he had to help us succeed."

The Yeerk said nothing. I think he knew he'd made an error. But I still sensed absolute confidence from him. Like a poker player holding an extra ace.

We reached the shack. It was a depressing, half-fallen-down mess with a wood floor and log walls and a roof that only covered half the place.

There was a bird's nest of some type in the rafters. Bushes had grown in through a hole in one wall. There were beer cans and soda cans strewn around, but they all looked pretty old. Nothing recent.

Tobias had chosen well. We would probably be left alone for the three days.

Tobias, with his laser vision, had found a few metres of rope in an old camp site. He flew back with it in his talons and Marco and Rachel tied my hands behind my back.

"Sorry, Jake," Marco said. "But that's the way it is. If you're still in there, you understand."

"We'll loosen the rope every couple of hours so the circulation isn't cut off," Rachel said. "I'll be here for the first shift. Cassie and Marco are going back with Ax, to get him prepared to play you." She smiled. "He already has the serious, responsible-sounding thing down. They just need to give him a sense of humour and stop him from playing with every sound he says."

It sounded fairly good to me. But I was nervous that only two of them would be around to guard me.

Of course, one of those two was Tobias. I could never run fast enough to hide from him. And Rachel could morph into a wolf and run me down.

But it bothered me that the Yeerk in my head had not lost his cockiness.

In fact, he was revelling in a fantasy of promotions and power. <Within a few hours I will be back with my kind. I will personally tell Visser Three all I know. It will be the end of your little band. The end! Visser Three will promote me again. It will be the fastest series of promotions ever. I'm already in the one-hundreds. I could rise to the nineties. I will be an Under-Visser. In a few of your years, who knows? I could be a Visser!>

But it was more than just talk. I could see the pictures, too. The images his mind conjured up. They were sketchy, but I saw Visser Three nodding his head as my Yeerk, still in my body, showed him my friends. They were all bound and gagged and lying helpless on the floor of Visser Three's Blade ship.

Why was I seeing this? The Yeerk was able to shield his other thoughts. Was this fantasy too emotional for him to hide from me? Or was he actually showing off for my benefit?

<Do you have these fantasies a lot?> I said, as cruelly as I could.

<You want to laugh at my fantasies? Shall I delve into a few of yours? Let's see what's hidden deep in your brain, human.>

And then, to my horror, I was no longer in the cabin. It was a bright, huge gymnasium. But not exactly a gym. A sports arena. Yes. With thousands and thousands of fans.

I felt like crawling away. I knew this fantasy. It was kind of lame, I guess. But I could not escape. The Yeerk could play my fantasies as easily as sticking a cassette into a video machine.

In my fantasy people were cheering. And there I was. In a pro uniform. I was older. But I still looked pretty much like myself.

The game clock was at five seconds. Four. Three. I set up and took an incredible three-point shot from mid-court.

Swish!

The stadium went crazy! Cheering. Horns sounding. People chanting my name.

And there was Cassie, in the stands. Smiling

at me. She was sitting with my parents.

And there was Tom.

He walked out on to the court and threw his arms around me. He patted me on the back.

"Great game," he said. "As usual."

End of fantasy. The images disappeared.

I felt very small suddenly. Very unimportant. Very weak.

<Ah, yes,> the Yeerk said, and laughed. <It shocks you that I can play your thoughts back for you. Your brain is no different to me than one of your primitive human computers. I open any file I like. I play any software. I use you. I own you. I dominate you. You are nothing any more. Just an echo. Just a ghost haunting the machine of your own brain!>

<Yeah?> I managed to say. <Well, you're a screw-up who is tied up in a cabin in the woods. In three days, you're dead.>

<I won't be here three days,> he said.

<You'll be here, far from your stinking Yeerk pool. No Kandrona rays. And you'll shrivel and die and crawl out of me.> I had been calm. But then, I lost control. <You'll die! You'll die like the others died! You think you'll win? You'll lose! You'll LOSE! You can't control me! You can't control me! You can't control me!>

<Oh?> the Yeerk asked with silky menace. <That's just what your brother said. At first. Shall

I show you? Shall I play one of Tom's memories for you? I can feel you cringe. I can feel your fear. Yes. Yes, I will. Here, enjoy a preview of your future.>

It was as if a third mind had joined us. It was real. So completely *real.* Not like a vision or a movie or something. I felt this. I *felt* it exactly as if I were there.

My brother's mind. His thoughts. His memories, as clear as if I were seeing them myself. Tom . . . some piece of Tom that the Yeerk still carried with him . . .

It was from just a few days earlier.

He was sitting at the breakfast table, across from me. I saw myself through his eyes. I looked . . . distant. Distracted. Preoccupied.

"Hey, midget. What's up?" he asked me.

"Not much. How about you?"

"Oh, I'm going to a meeting."

"The Sharing?" I asked him.

"Yeah. We're doing some clean-up in the park. You know, do our part for the community and all. Then we're having a barbecue afterwards. You really should join, you know. We'd get to spend more time together."

It was just as I remembered it. Except that now, I felt Tom's emotions, not mine.

The real Tom. The true Tom who was crushed beneath the Yeerk's control.

He was crying. Sobbing, helplessly, silently.

<Not Jake,> he cried. <Leave Jake alone. Leave my brother alone. I'll . . . look, I'll never trouble you again. I swear it. Just leave Jake alone.>

The Yeerk waited while the full impact of direct contact with Tom's mind sank into my own. Tom was defeated. Desperate. He spent his time wishing he could die.

He had given up any hope of escape. Given up.

<That's how it always is,> the Yeerk said. <At first the host fights, or at least tries. But hour after hour and day after day they see that they cannot rule their own bodies. The host sees that no one even knows what has happened to him. No one *knows* he is lost in his own head. And, over time, hope dies. The host becomes a faint, shattered creature. Like your brother.>

The Yeerk was telling the truth. That was what made it so terrible. It was true. I could feel Tom's complete, utter despair.

I could feel that he had accepted defeat.

I knew that all he wished for now was an end.

And I knew, also, that I was no stronger than Tom.

But still, one hope lingered in me. <Three

days,> I told the Yeerk. <In three days you will die.>

<Wait and see, human. Just wait and see.>

Chapter 21

I found out very late that first night why the Yeerk was so confident.

Rachel was keeping guard. Tobias was nearby in a tree.

They had brought food — some sandwiches and some juice, which "I" had eaten. Then, as Rachel sat nearby, reading a book by the light of a flashlight, the Yeerk pretended to sleep.

I guess in a way I did actually sleep. I was mentally exhausted. I was weary and depressed. More tired than I have ever been in my life. And yet afraid that if I dreamed, the Yeerk would watch my dreams.

My fear was justified. I did dream. The same dream I'd had before.

I was the tiger. Tom was my prey.

We were in the dark, deep woods, and I was hunting him with all my tiger skill. He was stumbling and noisy and weak.

I knew I would take him.

At last, too tired to run any further, Tom fell. He waited, helpless, while I gathered the power of my tiger body and prepared to leap . . .

And then, I was no longer the tiger. I was my own prey. I watched through eyes wide with terror as the tiger sprang.

I woke up. My eyes were already open.

<Interesting dream,> the Yeerk said. <Very metaphorical.>

I looked out through the eyes the Yeerk had opened. Rachel was still sitting back against the wall. Her book was open on her lap. But her breathing was heavy and regular. Her eyes were closed.

She had fallen asleep!

Her flashlight was still on. It shone across the rough wood floor. It illuminated my right arm and leg.

My arm . . . my leg . . . they had changed! My arms were thicker, more powerful, and growing larger still. My hands had swollen and become huge. The fingers were disappearing, replaced by curved claws as sharp as stilettos.

Orange-and-black-striped fur appeared, a rippling wave that grew to cover me.

I was becoming the tiger!

The realization hit me like a jolt of electricity. I was morphing!

The Yeerk was morphing!

How could I have been so stupid? Of course! The Yeerk controlled my hands and feet and voice, he controlled my very mind. Of course he had my morphing power, too!

The others . . . they didn't realize. They didn't understand. They had tied me up, but it was useless. The Yeerk had access to every one of my morphs.

The ropes around my hands were painfully tight as my wrists swelled to become powerful forepaws.

The Yeerk raised the rope and used the tiger's teeth to tear the rope apart.

I wanted to warn Rachel. She was still asleep. I had to warn her. The Yeerk would escape. He might even kill her.

But try as I might, I *could not* reach my own body any longer. I could not *reach* my own body.

<I won't kill her,> the Yeerk said. <Like you, she is capable of morphing. I will deliver Visser Three four morph-capable humans, as well as one Andalite scum.>

I now saw the world through tiger's eyes. The night was brighter. And I heard with tiger's ears.

Ears that caught any sound that might be made by a predator.

The tiger sniffed the air. But the breeze was slight, and carried no warnings.

<What a wonderful animal this is, this tiger,> the Yeerk said. <Excellent senses. Fast and silent and deadly.>

The forest was dark and quiet, but for the rustling of leaves in the trees above. Absolute silence, as the tiger crept away. No sound as the tiger melted into the shadows. And Rachel still slept.

Soon the shack could no longer be seen. The beam of Rachel's flashlight was swallowed by black night.

But the Yeerk was uncertain now. He did not know where we were. He did not know which way to go.

And then . . . a sound. A smell.

Humans!

<What are humans doing here?> He opened my memory. He searched my brain for an explanation. I had none. <Your own thoughts tell me it is wrong. It is very late. Humans, this deep in the forest?>

The Yeerk moved away from the human scent. They might be hunters. They might be park rangers. Those were the possibilities he had pulled from my own brain.

The Yeerk sent the tiger body into a loping run. But after just ten minutes, the tiger tired and he had to slow down. Tigers are not distance runners.

<Which way?> the Yeerk wondered.

And then . . . once again. Human scent. Human sounds.

I looked through the tiger's eyes and saw nothing. The Yeerk once more turned from the human scent.

The Yeerk searched my memory. <South. I must go south. But which way is south? Anything else will send me deeper into the forest.>

<I guess you're lost,> I said. The first thing I had said to the Yeerk in a long time.

<Shut up, slave. Once the sun rises in the morning I will know the way to go.>

<Two hours in a morph,> I reminded him. <If I'm stuck in tiger morph, then this body will be useless to you. Visser Three will want my body morph-capable.>

<Don't tell me what Visser Three wants,> the Yeerk said.

But the Yeerk knew time was passing. He had to morph back to my normal human shape.

Moments later, I was watching the world through human senses. The night vision was less acute. The ears heard too little. The human nose could scarcely smell a thing.

The Yeerk walked, pushing on as fast as my human body could move with no shoes.

<In a hurry to go nowhere?> I asked.

<I know where I'm going,> the Yeerk snapped. Then he stopped. <Hah! I should have thought of it. Of course! The falcon morph. I will simply fly away.>

I watched like it was a TV programme. Like I was far away from my own body. I watched with interest as the body shrank. As wings sprouted. As talons appeared. As —

WHAM!

The half-bird, half-human body went rolling, end over end across the ground.

<What?> the Yeerk demanded. <What hit me?>

He looked around frantically. But falcon eyes are for daytime hunting. They are stunningly good in sunlight. In the dark, they are nothing special.

The Yeerk continued to morph. Falcon feathers grew, the wings became more fully formed.

WHAM!

A shadow within shadows. A sense of something dark that disappeared before the Yeerk could turn the falcon's head. From far away I realized the falcon body had been injured. There was a deep, bloody gash in the right shoulder.

The Yeerk was beginning to be afraid.

WHAM!

A hammer blow! A ripping of flesh and tendon.

The invisible enemy had struck again. The falcon would not be able to take wing. Not now. The falcon was crippled. Disabled by a silent, invisible enemy.

And then I felt hope come alive in me again.

Because even as the Yeerk, crying in pain, demorphed and returned to human form, I saw the enemy.

It landed on a branch. It was outlined against faint moonlight and infrequent stars. The two little tufts on its head inspired its name.

<The great horned owl,> I said to the Yeerk.

<I can read your every thought, you don't need to tell me what it is,> the Yeerk snapped.

<Oh, but I enjoy telling you. It's a great horned owl. It flies without making a sound. Tobias watches them hunt sometimes. Tobias says they can hear a mouse burp from a hundred metres away. He says they can see a bug blink on a coal-black night.> I laughed silently in my corner of my own brain. I laughed at the Yeerk. <As far as that owl is concerned, you might as well have a spotlight on you.>

Then, to my amazement, Cassie's thought-speak was in my head. A voiceless voice that seemed to belong in a different life.

<Sorry I had to hurt you, Jake. But it was necessary. We realized the Yeerk would try morphing. So we were ready. Rachel only pretended to sleep. We wanted this Yeerk of yours to make his escape when we were most ready for him. So you hang in, Jake. The forest is full of your friends.>

The humans the tiger had smelled. . . My friends.

Then I felt it again. The sensation that filled me with a grim sort of pleasure. I felt the Yeerk's fear.

It was good to know that he was afraid.

It was very good.

Chapter 22

I could feel the Yeerk opening my memory like a book again. He was checking through the list of all the morphs I had ever done.

Dog. Fish. Flea. Seagull. Dolphin. Ant. Wolf.

I knew what he must be thinking. Which could he use to evade the watchful owl in the tree above us? The owl who saw through the night like it was day, and heard the sounds no human could hear.

<She can't stay in owl morph for ever,> the Yeerk said. <She has a two-hour time limit. Just as I do.>

<But of course there's Rachel and Marco and Ax. You don't know how many of them are here. You don't know where they are or what they are.>

<Can the owl watch a flea? I doubt it. Or an ant?> The Yeerk smirked.

<True. But how far can a flea travel in the two-hour time limit? Twenty metres? Thirty? Then you have to demorph and my friends will have no trouble finding you.>

<Shut up!> he yelled, losing patience.

I revelled in his anger. It meant he was scared. It also meant something else. I could not control my arms or legs. I could not even keep my mind closed from him. But he could not stop my thoughts. He could not stop me from talking to him.

And I had the power to annoy him. To distract him when he should be focused on escaping.

<You think you can harass me?> he said, reading my thoughts as soon as I had them. <You overestimate yourself.>

<You underestimate us, Yeerk. You thought you'd just morph and walk away. You guessed wrong. And your three days is less than two and a half already. Tick tock, Yeerk. Tick tock.>

<Let's see whether your owl friend can handle a wolf as easily as she handled the falcon.>

He began morphing. The wolf form was one I had enjoyed. Wolves are not subject to much fear. And their instincts are easily manipulated. Not like ants. Or the lizard that was one of my earliest morphs.

I watched as my body sprouted grey fur. As my face bulged out to become a long snout. As my ears slid up the side of my head to rest on top.

<I see our owl friend is keeping her distance,> the Yeerk said. <I thought as much.>

He set out at a fast trot. Unlike tigers, wolves are long-distance travellers. They can cover amazing distances at a run. And worse, the wolf brain seemed to have some interior sense of direction. It knew which way was deeper into woods, and which way led to the city.

We ran through woods, through a night as dark as night can be. Clouds hung low over the forest, allowing only the palest glow from the moon.

<A quick jog back to what passes for civilization on this planet, demorph to human, and your friends will be powerless to stop me,> the Yeerk said.

I wondered who he was trying to convince. Me, or himself?

<You're an arrogant bunch, aren't you? You Yeerks, I mean.>

<Arrogant? Why wouldn't we be? We are the most powerful race in the galaxy. Overlords of the Taxxons. Conquerors of the Hork-Bajir and the Ssstram and the Mak. Soon to be conquerors of the humans.>

<Don't count the humans just yet,> I said. <And there are still the Andalites.>

<We'll save the Andalites for last,> he hissed.

He stopped moving and pricked up his wolf's ears. There came a distinct howling sound. Loud and not very far away, it rose and warbled and rose again before dying away.

A second wolf voice howled.

<Another wolf. Two,> the Yeerk said. I felt him contact the wolf's own submerged instinctive mind. What was the meaning of the howling?

A notice. A warning to any other wolves that we are here. Don't come around, unless you want to risk a fight.

Suddenly I realized what it meant. I laughed.

<This is an area we were in before,> I said. <As wolves. We discovered —>

<Silence! I know what you found. When will you figure out that I can read your memory as well as you can?>

<We found another pack of wolves. They think this is *their* territory,> I went on, enjoying the fact that I was bothering him. <Those howls you hear? Those are my friends. They're calling to the other wolf pack. Better run faster, Yeerk. That big male who runs the other pack is tough.>

The Yeerk began running all out, pushing the wolf body for all the speed and endurance it had.

The dark tree trunks were a blur as we ran through the night, followed by the howls of wolves who were not wolves.

Then, a smell on the wind. The smell of another wolf. A male wolf.

<I believe that's my old friend now,> I said, laughing.

The Yeerk stopped running.

Ahead, through the trees, a pair of glittering yellow eyes glared at us. Other eyes appeared. Five wolves — five *real* wolves — waited for us to try to move forward.

<Go ahead,> I taunted the Yeerk. <Go for him. Of course, that's a *real* wolf there. An alpha male. Leader of his pack, which means he's probably been in a dozen fights and won them all. Go on, Yeerk. Tell him how the Yeerks are masters of the galaxy. I'm sure he'll be very impressed.>

I could sense the Yeerk's hesitation. His uncertainty.

<So many species on this planet,> he said to himself. <So many balances and connections. Everything preying on everything else. Every power is checked by some other power. Every advantage is cancelled by some disadvantage.>

<Yeah. Earth. It's a tough neighbourhood.>

<When we take this planet, we will eliminate these species. We will simplify. Things should

be simpler. Yes, much simpler.>

<I have a news flash for you, Yeerk. I don't think you're going to take this planet. I think this planet is going to take you.>

Just then, a human voice. "So. You about done playing games? Ready to come back to the shack?"

It was Marco. He was shoeless and wearing his morphing outfit. He had been one of the wolves who'd led us straight into the enemy pack.

Marco shivered. "Look, Mr Yeerk, it's cold and I'm freezing. I always knew this situation with the morphing outfits was going to be trouble some day. So come on. Let's go back to the shack."

For a moment the Yeerk was so enraged he was ready to leap at Marco and tear out his throat.

But then, lumbering up behind Marco came Rachel. The very large version of Rachel with the trunk, the big leathery ears, and the two huge tusks.

Marco seemed to guess what had gone through the Yeerk's mind. "Go ahead. Try something. A wolf pack ahead. A very large, surprisingly fast African elephant behind you. And more surprises in the woods all around you. Oh, and one more thing . . . Cassie is nestled down in your fur. Sucking your blood, I imagine. She did the flea thing."

I realized then that there is a very basic difference between Yeerks and humans.

A human will fight even when he knows he can't win. Maybe our species is just a little crazy. But human history is full of cases where a handful of guys would fight an entire army. They'd get stomped, but they'd fight anyway.

That's not the way it is for Yeerks. They are ruthless. They will do anything, absolutely anything to win. But when the situation is impossible, totally impossible, they stop fighting. They figure that other Yeerks will carry on the fight for them.

Different ways of looking at your world.

<You are fools,> the Yeerk said, having read my thoughts. <It is madness to fight when you cannot win.>

<Yes, it is foolish. It is crazy,> I agreed. <And it's why we will win.>

The Yeerk demorphed and returned to human form. *My* human form.

Marco walked away into the woods. Rachel rumbled off. And a few minutes later, an owl appeared to lead the way back to the shack.

Chapter 23

The next morning, when it seemed like no one was watching, the Yeerk tried again. He morphed into an ant. He got a metre before running into a group of ants from a different colony. About forty of them attacked. They were ripping the ant body apart when the Yeerk de-morphed and returned to human form.

<This is a savage planet,> he said. <We will tame this world, when we take it over.> But I don't think even he believed it any more.

It was around nine in the morning on Saturday that the Yeerk first took over my body and brain. By Monday evening, when the sun went down, he was growing distracted, unable to concentrate clearly.

By the time the moon rose in a newly clear, starry sky, he was weak with hunger. His slug body cried out for Kandrona rays the way a human would cry for food or water.

I could feel his arrogance evaporate. I could feel his despair.

He still had fantasies of being rescued. But he couldn't make those fantasies end very well. Even if he was rescued, he would no longer be the big hero who had destroyed the Animorphs.

He would try to think of clever ways to outwit my friends, but he could never be sure who was in the woods around us. Or what form they might have taken.

He tried to take on a bird shape again, reforming the peregrine falcon. The DNA had not been affected by the injuries Cassie had caused to the earlier morph, of course. The falcon was fine. But it was daylight this time, and Tobias landed while the falcon was still half-morphed. He grabbed the falcon head in his talon and simply explained that if the Yeerk did not demorph, he would be killed.

For the first time, the Yeerk broke his silence with the others and spoke as a Yeerk.

<If you kill me, you'll kill your friend, as well,> he warned.

<Yes,> Tobias said. <I know.>

<You won't do it.>

<Right from the start we have all said the same thing — better to die than be a Controller,> Tobias said. <But in any case, I don't need to kill you. I can simply put your eyes out. A blind falcon doesn't fly far.>

The Yeerk surrendered and demorphed.

We waited, as the minutes and hours of the night ticked away. He still hoped for a miracle to save him. But his hunger was a terrible thing, growing with every second.

<You think you'll win,> he sneered at me. <You won't win. Your people are blind to what is happening. And the Andalites will not return in time.>

<Maybe. But you won't be there to see it,> I said. <It must be four in the morning. Five hours left. Tick tock.>

<You're a cruel little human, aren't you?>

<I don't think so, no.>

<You know I am dying and you laugh at me.>

<What do you expect? Pity?>

He laughed. <No. We don't offer pity. And we don't expect pity. We are the masters of the galaxy. Conquerors of the Hork-Bajir and — >

<Yeah, yeah, I know. The mighty Yeerk empire.>

After that he said nothing to me for a while. It was impossible to sleep. He sat with my eyes open. He was too hungry to rest. The hunger infiltrated his mind. It twisted his thoughts.

<The Yeerk home world is a simpler place than this planet. Simple and elegant. No more than a hundred animal species. What do you have on Earth? A million species? More? What does a planet need with a million species?>

I didn't answer. His time was running out. Let him talk.

<We Yeerks evolved as parasites, not predators. Unlike you humans, we did not kill to eat. We were peaceful. We took many different species as our hosts. And as they evolved, so did we. Over time, the Gedds evolved. They were a sort of . . . like a monkey, I suppose. We were in the Gedds till the Andalites first came. Some of our people still have nothing better than Gedds for hosts.>

<What about the Andalites?> I asked. <What happened when they came to your world?>

<Of course. The Andalite has not told you their story, has he? What a pity. It's such a fine story. Ask your pet Andalite Ax sometime. Ask him about the story of the Andalites and the Yeerks.>

<Maybe I will,> I said. I hoped the Yeerk would keep talking, but he fell silent.

The hours passed. An owl left and was replaced by another. The moon went down. Dawn was coming. I could feel it.

<Yes,> the Yeerk said, having read my

thoughts. <Dawn. Just a few hours left. Ahhhh!> He cried out in silent pain. <The fugue. It begins.>

<The fugue?>

<The final hours. You will not enjoy it, although you may learn a great deal, human. You may learn more than you want to — *aaaahhh!*>

I was watching his pain from far away. I was an observer. Close enough to know what he was feeling, but feeling none of it myself.

At first it was wave after wave of pain. Starvation and death by thirst. All rolled into one agony.

The sun came up. Cassie stepped into the shack from the woods outside. She looked at me and nodded. "It's happening, isn't it?"

I wanted to answer, but even now, my voice was not my own.

Cassie came and sat down beside me. Beside us.

"Ax says this part is pretty rough. Just remember, when it's all over, I'll be here."

She slipped her hand into my hand. I could feel it. So could the Yeerk. But he did not reject this small bit of comfort, even though it was intended for me and not him.

His mind was deteriorating. His thoughts were becoming more visible to me. Like a movie that kept drifting in and out of focus.

I saw images from a strange place, as seen

through strange eyes. Liquid all around. Shapes, like squids, shooting through the liquid. Yeerks. Swimming in the Yeerk pool. Soaking up Kandrona rays.

And there were images of the first host. A Gedd. So, I thought — that's what a Gedd looks like. I had seen a few aboard the Yeerk mother ship but had not known what they were. They were humanoid, short and stooped, with webbed feet and three clumsy fingers.

I saw the world as the Yeerk had seen it, through Gedd eyes. The vision was dim. The hearing was better. The Yeerk had been excited at getting his first host. He had subdued the Gedd mind with ruthless ease, crushing it with his superior intelligence and will.

The memory made me sick. The Gedd's bewilderment. His fear. And the Yeerk's fierce arrogance.

I turned my attention away from the memory and back to the world around me. To my surprise, I noticed that my arms were shaking. My legs were shaking.

Cassie had put her arm around my shoulders.

"Jake, if you can hear me, it's almost eight. One hour to go. Jake . . . the Yeerk in your head is dying."

"Yes," I wanted to say. "He is."

Chapter 24

The fugue.

The final hours of the Yeerk's life. I was watching him die.

A lot has happened to me since I first saw the Andalite prince land in that construction site. More strange things than happen to most people in their entire lives. But the strangest was this. And the saddest.

The Yeerk cried in pain, again and again. And the visions came floating up, crystal clear, as if they had just happened.

Visions of the good times in the Yeerk's life. And of bad times. The emotions were strange. Alien. I guess that's the word for them. There was no memory of love. I guess Yeerks don't do love. But there was affection. Pride. Fear. Regret. Those I could understand.

And along with the Yeerk's own memories, I began to see the minds of his hosts. The Gedd who had a name no human could hope to pronounce. The Hork-Bajir warrior who had fought the Yeerk in his head every day of his life.

The Hork-Bajir, who had been forced to attack his own kind, to destroy his own friends, as an unwilling slave of the Yeerks.

But it was more than just memories. It was more. The Yeerk had carried with him some small part of that Hork-Bajir warrior's being.

Like a computer transferring a document on to a floppy disk, I realized. Part of the Gedd and part of the Hork-Bajir had been transferred permanently to the Yeerk.

And to my shock, I knew that those parts were now being transferred to me.

And then . . . the memories I feared most.

Tom.

He had joined The Sharing for a simple, silly reason. A pretty girl he liked was a member. He had wanted to get close to her. He had gone to meetings. He'd played along with them, never guessing the truth. All he had cared about was the girl.

He had stumbled, accidentally, into a secret leadership meeting. He thought the girl was seeing another boy. But she was one of them.

He had followed her, wandered into the meeting and seen Visser Three. Visser Three in his Andalite body.

I saw the Controllers grab a yelling, punching, kicking Tom. I saw as they tied him up. Carried him through secret passageways to the great, underground Yeerk pool.

I saw him scream as he realized what was happening. I felt his fear. I felt his rage as the Yeerk slug crawled into his ear and wrapped itself around his brain. I felt every ounce of his despair.

And like the Gedd and the Hork-Bajir, this human, my brother, became a part of me.

The Yeerk was no longer in pain. It was beyond pain.

I opened my eyes and looked at Cassie. It happened so naturally. I opened my eyes. By my own will.

I don't know how she knew, but I guess she did. She nodded slightly and met my gaze.

For the first time in more than an hour, the Yeerk spoke. <So. You win . . . human.>

The Yeerk shuddered. I could feel it. A physical spasm. My vision changed. I felt . . . it's hard to describe. I felt as if I were seeing through things. *Into* things. Like I could see the front and back and top and bottom and inside of everything all at once.

And then I saw it.

A creature. Or a machine. Some combination of both. It had no arms. It sat still, as if unable to move, on a throne that was kilometres high.

Its head was a single eye. The eye turned slowly . . . left . . . right . . .

I trembled. I prayed it would not look my way.

And then it saw me.

The eye, the blood-red eye, looked straight at me.

It saw me.

It SAW me!

No! NO! I cried in silent terror. I looked away.

And when I opened my eyes again, all I saw was a weird glow.

The glow faded, little by little.

I was trembling.

"It's over, Jake," Cassie said.

I rose slowly to my feet. I moved my own legs. I was in control of myself again.

I looked down on the wooden floor of the shack.

A grey slug, not fifteen centimetres long, lay there . . . still.

As we watched, it withered and shrivelled and became nothing.

Chapter 25

"Jake? Are you all right, sweetheart?" my mum asked me that night at dinner.

I looked up. I'd been staring at my food, I realized. Something with pasta and tuna fish.

"What?" I asked.

My mum and dad exchanged one of their "worried parent" looks. "Well, you're not eating. Don't you like it?"

I shrugged. "Sorry. It's fine. I was just . . . distracted."

My dad nodded. "It's just a change from the last two nights. You've been eating like you were trying to eat everything in the house."

"I was?"

Tom cocked an eyebrow at me. "What, now

you're going to pretend it didn't happen? Last night you sat here and ate six pieces of chicken and kept yapping about how great it was. Then you ate a pie. A pie which was supposed to be for the four of us."

I hid a smile. Of course. Ax. The Andalite had played me for three days — two hours at a time. Ax was dangerous around food. The sense of taste was still totally amazing to him. When he was in human morph you didn't want to get between him and a bar of chocolate. Or a pie, I guess.

"You were a total pig," Tom said. "Chicken. Corn. Potatoes. Or, as you kept saying, 'Potatoes. Toes. Tay-toes.' I thought you'd gone nuts."

And were you suspicious, Yeerk? I thought, looking at my brother. A new Yeerk was in Tom's head. Another arrogant master of the galaxy.

My brother was trapped in a small corner of his own mind, able to see and feel, but powerless to do a thing. I knew.

I didn't sleep much that night. I did not want the dreams to come. I feared terrible nightmares of the eye. The eye that had stared at me from a different universe.

But the only dream that came was a familiar one.

I was the tiger. My brother was the prey. But, in the end, I was my brother. And he was me.

On the news that night there was a small

report on the closing of the new hospital. There was no explanation. But I knew what had happened. The Yeerks knew their plan was blown. They understood that we knew about it.

We had hurt them pretty badly.

But I knew better than to celebrate. Visser Three would be more determined than ever to stop us.

The next day I did something stupid. At least, Marco kept telling me it was stupid. But he didn't object very much. He understood.

We all met at Cassie's barn. And I used her dad's cellular phone to call Tom at home. I went partly into a wolf morph before I did. Just enough to make the smallest changes.

Enough to change the shape of my mouth and tongue and throat. So that my voice would sound very different.

He picked it up on the third ring. "Yeah?"

"I have a message," I said in a thick, twisted voice that did not sound at all like me.

"What?" Tom asked.

"Don't give up, Tom. Don't ever give up."

I hung up before he could say anything.

"Do you think Tom . . . the real Tom . . . heard it?" Rachel asked.

"He heard," I answered.

I wondered if he would have the strength to hold on.

But I knew the answer. See, a part of my brother was in my own mind now. Along with echoes of a long-dead Hork-Bajir and a simple Gedd. And yes, even a bit of a Yeerk with dreams of glory.

Marco smiled his sardonic smile. "And is it true? Will we win?"

"This is a very complicated planet, Marco. That's what I hear, anyway. And it's a very strange universe. Anything could happen."

Reader beware – you choose the scare!

Give Yourself Goosebumps

A scary new series from R.L. Stine – where you decide what happens!

1 Escape From the Carnival of Horrors
2 Tick Tock, You're Dead!
3 Trapped in Bat Wing Hall
4 The Deadly Experiments of Dr Eeek
5 Night in Werewolf Woods

Choose from over 20 scary endings!